D1108960

1

The Affair

Rita EL KHAYAT

The Affair

Novel

Edited and translated by Peter Thompson

By the same author

Le Monde Arabe au Féminin, 3rd edition, L'Harmattan, Paris, 1988
Le Maghreb des Femmes, Eddif, Casablanca, 1992
Le Somptueux Maroc des Femmes, Dedico, Salé, 1994
Une Psychiatrie Moderne pour le Maghreb, Santé Cultures Collection, Paris, 1994
Les Sept Jardins, L'Harmattan, Paris, 1995
La Folie. El Hank. Casablanca, Eddif, Casablanca, 2000
Le Livre des Prénoms du Monde Arabe, 4th edition, Eddif, Casablanca, 2001
Le Maghreb des Femmes, 2nd edition, Marsam, Rabat, 2001
Le Somptueux Maroc des Femmes, 2nd edition, Marsam, Rabat, 2002

Originally published in Paris, by Editions L'Harmattan, with title *La Liaison,* and under the pseudonym Lyne Tywa (2000). Later published in Morocco, copyright 2002, Casablanca (ISBN 9954-8153-0-9), by Editions Aïni Bennaï, (also Casablanca, 2006).

© L'Harmattan, 2018
5-7, rue de l'École-Polytechnique, 75005 Paris
http://www.editions-harmattan.fr
ISBN : 978-2-343-14538-9
EAN : 9782343145389

Translator's Note

This is the anguished story of a young woman and an older man, and the way their vulnerabilities fail (not always, but in the end) to complement each other ideally. The ideal is constantly hinted at, and the physical is often transcended. But it is a story of failure and loss.

The book that first appeared under a pseudonym—shockingly erotic for a tale purported to be the *cri de coeur* of a woman from a Muslim country—was written with pen on paper in 1985. Its Moroccan author was temporarily in Spain—the Andalusia that is so often echoed in Moroccan and Algerian writing. She had been emerging from long repression—Freudian and cultural—and exploring the "mutilation," as she says, of her "instinctive-affective sphere." Marguerite Duras's *The Lover* (*L'Amant*) opened the way, she adds, for some of this book's tone and its psychological accuracy.

It is a book—a fitful avowal, really—that continually reasserts itself in and through cultures, because through all its incarnations (including the Italian translation in 1996) it was expurgated five times by Rita El Khayat. It is hard to know what shocked whom, or might have, in different readerships, or what the author removed in order to achieve an exact balance of the physical and the metaphysical. The original pseudonym was Lyne Tywa, an inversion of the protagonist's name. The book appeared in France in 1995 under this pseudonym, and in Morocco under El Khayat in 2006.

The only other English translation of El Khayat is *Open Correspondence*, a collection of the letters between her and the great Moroccan writer and critic Abdelkébir Khatibi (University of New Orleans Press, Engaged Writers Series, 2010). The veiled and spiritual rapport those two writers developed was given the name *aimance* by Khatibi. Those letters were perhaps a signal toward El Khayat's preferred language of the heart. So, too, are her stories in *Les Sept Jardins*. Critical attention could profitably focus on the Arab and Berber traditions behind these stories, and the relation of their classicism to *The Affair's* metaphysical aura. At the appearance of the latter book, amid loud commentary on its eroticism, critic Charles Bonn noted El Khayat's "assertion of classicism" (*classicisme affirmé*).

Rita El Khayat is a psychiatrist, critic and editor and, in her role as publisher and frequently-invited speaker, an agent and spokesperson of Moroccan culture. At times this role reasserts the primacy of Berber tradition. Increasingly, she is seen as one of Morocco's indispensable feminists. Not a voguish one, but one who speaks from a psychiatric background, and out from under Arab patriarchal norms. In the Western world we often forget that the Berbers were in North Africa before the Arabs.

So passages both beguile and disgust, through sordid trysts in what the protagonist calls "the slum"—but these moments are laid next to passages of soaring mysticism. This story is not just enigmatic, ornate in places—like much story-telling in Arab tradition. It deliberately sets a woman's (or her narrator's) raw admissions against a male figure who is self-centered and essentially (not just for the reader!) unknowable. While the woman's admissions, and her reflections on her younger self, are searingly self-analytical (could anyone but a psychiatrist have written this?), the foil of the unknowable older man leads us to the edge of the metaphysical. I was careful to confirm this intent in a meeting with the author. Echoes of ancient Berber culture (Tywalyne, Berber for "my eyes") draw us up to a level—

abstract, spiritual—that floats above the story line. Even the brevity and condensation of this tale suggest that it is a philosopher's stone for something *other*: a meditation not only on love but on the passage of time and the ability to know.

Many of El Khayat's works reinforce this leaning. What is remarkable is that this epistemological note is rung above a quavering ontology whose flesh is desperate sex in a slum apartment—whose self-assertion is as halting and difficult as any of the events of "the affair."

Ifrane, Morocco, 2016

Foreword

This novel belongs to a woman, Tywalyne. The word is Moroccan Berber and means "My Eyes," and by extension of these organs' refinement, and the refinement of all their mythology and importance, it signifies Love. So the meaning is a syncretic one.

In Moroccan Arabic a different organ has long had the meaning "my love," and, strangely, it's the liver...—or "little liver" in moments (both Arabic and Berber) of tenderness.

Tywalyne is not really a first name, but its lush sound and its esthetic and affective weight perfectly suit our heroine...

May despondent souls find no more than a fiction wrapped around these outbursts of love, and may those who are captured by the game contemplate only their own selves, their own "I"...

Tywalyne tells the story as "I," and that may shock—for the reality of this loving violence will embarrass all kinds of transfixed and shameful lovers, as it drags them through feelings that are confused, troubled, troubling.

This text is an allegory of the gaze, while keeping in mind that the little god of love shoots his arrows blindfolded.

Love is blind.

Prologue

Tywalyne, a bit later on, will marry the man she loves and through whom she has lived a thousand deaths. She conceives a child, finally, a child dramatically lost before birth. Complications from this event leave her forever sterile...

Chapter 1

I was twenty. I was very beautiful, and had no idea. I knew nothing. Then I was thirty, thirty dilapidated and stunted years under that flag of all neurasthenic women going through confused times, the moment they have decided to say goodbye to men. Then forty drew near, when I met that Man at a high arc of age, but not a high point in my life: I was thirty-five. He who never told me his age, never left an ID card or any document lying around, is at least ten years older. It works for me. Or it did. Now, he's old. Which means he can no longer be the subject of such a violent love…

We drew nearer each other for three years, still distant, like sinking boats that think they see the lighthouse among the waves while it drops more surely than ever from sight.

When we speak of first times, we usually think of the bed: sheets, dampness. For me, the first time was a meeting place—of destiny, fire, cremation.

Certain scattered memories, too scorching to fade, remind me that the main thing is I was so much younger when I first met him. This is a chunk of my life that I've tried to file away somewhere, and it now seems I've done everything possible to stuff it into a past as black as squid ink.

I was perhaps twenty-eight, and when we were first introduced I was as low as could be on the scale of social graces. The fact is I was crushed by his cool importance… In this respect the only difference between us is that I've never stopped growing and refining myself, while he is static, content with his immense privileges, the kind that are born out of a cold conscience. It's worth pointing out that many empty, mean, dull people fashion themselves a social reality by means of this ever-present and malicious affectation: *I exist mainly to crush people because I am the only one that counts.* That's what these (yes, in the end, hateable) men and women seem to be saying.

And in fact I found him hateable. I felt an aversion. He appeared badly dressed, with the general look of a failed soccer player putting on his best suit when he has to meet people he fears as powerful and important. At his home I was really awful, not greeting anyone, retreating to a corner and thinking about so many moments of my life starting to sift through my fingers like the sand you try to hold onto, the last days of August, on the beach. Who would have thought that one day, bound up in the chimera I'd become, languid and well entertained, I could swoon in these very surroundings and in the arms of this man?

I largely forgot him, yet my memory held something—a sharp annoyance whenever I thought of him.

And then, as reality would have it, I had to see him again. Him. My irritation grew along with my intuition that the balance of power was not in my favor. It's still that way, and that won't go away unless I succeed in killing off all feelings for him.

I had prepared, having some sense of the shock I was in for. Grey flannel, grey silk, black crocodile bag, grey scarf, grey footwear with grey stockings, and my legs just pressing together but not crossed—a habit I find revolting in women. The grey silk of my legs was indecent. I had knowingly conjured femininity with this dizzy swirl of greys and blacks. A perverse femininity that only a roué would sniff out. Intuitively I was exactly centered in his own tone, his desire. When he showed up, thinking to rush through the appointment, something in his eyes, in less than a second, and in what seemed an "above suspicion" freezing of his body, told me that he was suddenly alert and thrown off track.

16

I re-entered a kind of arena. Unconsciously I had let myself lose the purpose of our meeting. One of us had somehow transformed these moments into man-and-woman moments. One of every pair is always destined for failure in flights of fancy and the emotions of love, which is to say the stirrings and floodings of the soul are very different, between both actors in the same love. It's usually the woman who lives out her passion in pain.

Staring into his pupils I realized that some overt desire or love was starting to make itself known. Feeling like an animal about to be slaughtered, I had the crazy memory that I had been told many times never to look a man in the eyes. Starting with my father. Prohibitions stay in us, inscribed, and only resurface suddenly in situations we're brutally thrust into without warning.

Confusion is the only way to describe it. My ambitions, yet again, had to get by a masculine referee. He was listening. Our talk was absurd, and behind it another talk held forth, preliminary and playful. In terms of the tacit preamble, it was clear that strength and decisiveness were in his hands alone.

In the room my voice stirred up warm waves and swells of silk. I had noticed this before, and more: my voice could really pin an audience back when I let it vibrate—it could enchant a child through story, and genuinely move an emaciated friend, a woman I might hang out with all afternoon (these occasions exist among women, like a necessity of womanhood). You learn these things the way you learn to breathe or move, you learn to sacrifice to social usage.

I had forgotten the lordliness of my voice; otherwise I would have seen why this man was listening with such attention and acuity in his eyes. A voice is always beautiful when it is sincere or true.

He reminded me of someone, several people. I let myself be pierced by his gaze and I think he violated me with his eyes, right there, six feet away from me. He didn't violate me. I gave in, and made long, voluptuous love with him, with the troubling certainty that one day he'd be my lover. His face had the sadness of an English aristocrat dying of the plague in a Venice given over to pestilence and death. And for long afterwards he'd keep this look of a love beggar, but in reality a beggar who can't say "thank you" and is even less capable of receiving the gift.

His gaze of extreme modesty combined with monstrous sensuality was like that of the peoples of the South as they hurled themselves toward Eldorados, poor renegades pinned to the sky of artificial paradises and new worlds.

Intelligence, considerable intelligence, at times overpowering, blossomed in his eyes in magnificent floods and waves. Is there anything more fascinating than a man of superior intelligence? This lovely intelligence stood out in every aspect of his being. Every trait. Something of overriding importance to my life was now in play in this meeting. As for him, he simply played at soaking in this woman so unlike all the others in his life: the army of young girls, old bags, and lucky evenings. That wasn't me, he could tell, and that alone kept him sitting there, held in my gaze. His eyes were a precipice. They said it all. While understanding all.

Since then, even with intense effort I've never been able to remember what we talked about.

It was on that day that I first gauged the incredible power of the human gaze: it can express anything. Any resistance I had to philosophy or optical science had crumbled. I have never since communicated with anyone in this sense—that there was no mask or charade I could hold up against his knowing incursions.

He had visited, in his way, my insides. Carried away by the tide of this intrusion, I knew that between us there was going to be an adventure, an adventure of our bodies, dubious and ineffable meetings played out in the headlong violence of the flesh...

Unfortunately, it would be accompanied by a love too real.

You must never look a man in the eyes...

We said goodbye like adolescents. Like teenagers who haven't had an adolescence, we were about to enclose ourselves in something for years to come, for long afternoons, to live out what life had forbidden us at the age of insouciance and complete openness. We separated that day—he was a bit timid but daring. Me, hunched in a hidden reserve, with that courtesy we have in life's great unexpected moments, in an attempt to make up for the wreckage already foretold by this rendezvous.

No matter how intimate your confessions, there are some you can never make without deforming them.

So I won't say how he took his leave... I was already suffering; I didn't want to see what his absence would feel like. My movements to get up and go somewhere were robotic, and I was invaded by contradictory, bitter-sweet, sensations.

I saw him again. The same place. Two or three times. We even spent four or five hours together, the last day of 1980. Night fell on our words. He ended up telling me most of his life story. I was flattened by the tale of his boyhood. I had rarely felt so much pain, reacting to someone's suffering. He told me he enjoyed my company, and, in all the years after, this was a truth he never once denied.

I knew he was married to an ever-present virago, as poor a mate for him as a mule is for a thoroughbred. I believed my judgment of her was fair, as I'd noticed her years before. So, was I already getting jealous, without quite realizing it? She had taken over him just as worms can own the most precious wood. Rotted through by her tireless, underground work, he would never be able to soar without collapsing.

The situation hurled me forward into my own fragility and despair. The thing is, I've never really wanted to live...

Of these three or four encounters, I only left him once with a sense of triumph. The first time, perhaps? The other times I left in pieces, hating people, life and despair—my lot, once again. I was powerless, and he was going to make me reach—again and again—the very bottom of this feeling of complete powerlessness.

Without planning it, we ended up on the same plane home, that frozen dawning of 1981, above snowy mountains, silent, immortal. Hanging in a bubble, or perhaps it was in a warm wind, warm as burning tea, sweet to the throat of those thirsting for tenderness.

We kept on talking. We didn't touch each other—that was too dangerous. Playing with fire.

I felt I was the only one losing her mind... We were profoundly seduced by each other. At each new meeting he was brand new, and I was too. His requirement was that we meet only when both of us were in impeccable shape. Attractive. And healthy. Perfect.

The following disappearance was to last a year and a half. What I felt for this man, a warm sloshing in my chest, the picture of his sad eyes forever fixed in my head, didn't go away. My connection to him was nothing more or less than biding time, before living again.

And I, fooled as always, went on for a long time thinking that it was over, this adventure that hadn't even started.

I don't know how it happened that we both took the same turn, when, at the beginning of 1981, I was about to choose a trip either to an island to rediscover the Tropics and their illusion of revival, or to the North and the falsehoods and myths of its luxurious, velvety cinemas, or to the mountains in their purple twilight. I had chosen to go look at the snow, far off in the high reaches, caking the mountain chains in eternal white...

Once back home, I tackled life's myriad busy-ness.

I'm sure it's in advanced age that men and women finally take the measure of the most intense and epochal things they have lived through. It's not ordinary people and things that add up to the immensity of our individual fate. It is peopled and composed of everything we could never let go of, everything that has still gnawed our bones, wrinkled our skin and left the heart heavy. With our grey hairs we know what we should have done, and what we've never been able to do.

I spent a year and a half or two in a completely morose state punctuated by a few magnificent partings in the clouds. I'm stunned by my passivity, and my innumerable failures fill me with disgust. I perfected a role for two years, its perfection absolute, silent and hidden from view.

And then one day I was told someone, X, had called and left contact information. We saw each other again. He wanted to know, methodically, a year and a half after the fact, everything I had done. Our meeting was as cordial as ever, long and, as usual, seeming to lack real portent—but with delights barely glimpsed, never reachable.

Instead I should have imagined it all as volcanic—the terrain, the temperature, and the explosive possibilities of expression. Lava that would flow only sporadically, sweat, saliva, tears, blood, and full-throated laughter. And his smiles—his equanimity. Seduction.

Coffee strong, then cold, ice water and the print of my lips on the glass...

Is it my boldness, that of an outspoken woman, or his shy person's clumsiness that brought about the knotty problem of how to see each other outside this neutral spot or on an airplane? I no longer know. This man has cost me all my landmarks.

The contest was insidious, sharp, and very clearly to his advantage. I gradually noticed he was getting the impression that there was nothing scary about me. All women are terrifying for him. And I... I give in to whatever he decides, so... I am The Only One. She who can be bruised without risk or resort of any kind. Everything suggests that men and women are really wrestling with each other even as they say how much they're in love—and melt in their partners' arms. It's not only a lie, but a lure that you wake up to one day, old and bent.

Nor do I belong to that cohort of glamor types that you want to nail to a bed an hour after meeting them. Nor to the contingent who know how to talk like little girls, or like languid maid servants.

Some have claimed I'm like a young man, or that I'm attracted to women. A few (two or three?) were staggered by my body's beauty, when they'd bared it, stripped it...—and this includes my doctor who shamelessly said he would have liked to eat it "on a skewer"—(which kind of makes you ponder the wiles of our physicians and enlightens us on their ferocity, their cloudy desires, and exactly what type of gaze they drape on our nakedness).

Their eyes are drowned in desire, those who have trouble looking at an undressed woman moving in painful or at least awkward ways.

As for this man, he was giving me his address on a doorstep when suddenly it sprang, from deep in me

"Is it possible you are—you are—available?"

He quickly saw what I was after, and his deep sense of protection lashed me with a curt "No." One word. I stuck out my hand, and stepped out, blinded by the light, in a complete turmoil. What was left for me to do, in all the hours to come, to keep from withering away? A boundless sadness had unfurled over me like a disaster's spreading tide. A feeling that was my age-old companion.

That desire to affirm something with him cost me another year and a half without a word. Without a call. And, naturally, with no recourse.

So when he called a year and a half later it had been eight years. During three of those years we'd spoken at great length, and for a year and a half we'd almost stumbled on risky ground together. I was overjoyed at his call, at the very time that a valley of tears was yawning before me. But hope, as strong as a religion, had come surging back. Still... I should have disappeared, let myself go to seed, locked myself away, the day that he inquired, at our second meeting, whether Monsieur T was my lover? I was choking with bitterness, that a man could use the formal "*vous*" addressing me, while searching in my eyes and asking point-blank

"Monsieur T... is he your lover?"

23

Of all the women I knew were in his life, I didn't have the absurd curiosity to know if, in each case, he was their lover. None of that mattered to me...

It was the alarm of a sinister calamity. He was jealous, in an unhealthy way. He would never bring it out in the open, preferring to hate rather than to know that this morbid sentiment is found in lots of people, impotent people who can't love with sincere oblativity, who love only the central wound of not being the only ones on earth. This massive insecurity drives the jealous mad—makes them mean, and disastrous.

The summer of 1983 began with the call I was no longer waiting for, and I'd forgotten everything, so vapid, gray and lost was my existence. Our story had become a dead-end path, aborted. The rare times when I thought of him during this long absence, I felt hurt, as if I'd given in to some childish moments with him. Those kinds of touches, between little boys and girls, not recognized for what they are, but electric and very instinctual—between children on the playground, between brothers and sisters left by themselves. Caresses, or fantasies of tendernesses and something more, a soaring toward the deep, the impossible.

We decided to meet on Sunday afternoon. I was burning up in my car, the city was empty and the heat crushing; he was tired and icy. I had already come to that spot, a few years before. He gave me something to drink (coffee, of course) used his handkerchief, sat down facing me, and began to stare. He was completely unlike the image I had of him. I was disoriented, irritated, and alarmed.

Only now do I realize that he's a composite beast, this chimera that haunts me. Lynx, jackal, wolf and fox—he's all these at once. A carnivore that catches everything with a piercing, cruel eye, that gobbles carrion, capable of tearing other lives to shreds to prolong his own life, and endowed with an obsessive intelligence. It's against the latter that I had collapsed like a bird crashing into the windshield, or those insects instantly exploding in blood when hit by a speeding car.

My masochism revealed itself to me like a photograph developing in a chemical bath. But I staggered on.

So I arrived, still uneasy that he was inviting me to his place. The triumphal summer went well with the white décor of his living room. In an ill-defined way, my nervousness lingered. He listened, watchful, the slightest smile on his face, from time to time just barely raising an eyebrow.

I wasn't sitting there figuring out how this duel would end. Nothing has ever prepared me for duels or even for defensive attitudes. For me, the Eden of man's first day still reigned on earth, every man and every woman was simply an Adam or Eve, deeply taken with the other in a lovely world, the scene of magic loves, necessary and translucent.

Two years later, I still ask myself if he had invited me there to take me, like a girl, over the back of one of the sofas. An honorable escape presented itself in the form of an unexpected visitor. He asked me if I'd like to be introduced. I fled through the kitchen under the eyes of an expressionless maid. I was far from the ease of those women so used to having affairs. Whatever I've lived—not counting this man—I've gone through it in broad daylight. I used to despise, and hotly despise—in what other life, now that I think about it, after what I went through with him?—those women who would hop on a plane and go spread their fat, frustrated thighs, to get away from their gray lives. In any case, at the time my life was not anything exciting; I was married rather to other kinds of speculation, not at all of the flesh, more ethereal and far from any sense of the real. But reality, unfortunately, catches up with the dreamiest and the most delicate to shove their noses in the stench of the material.

He was to call again, sometimes pursuing me, inadvertently, right at the moment that I was regaining a little peace. Over two years of our connection I received one phone call for every three promised. I repeatedly threatened to leave him, which never yielded anything but this:

"Do it!"
or more often:
"That's the best thing you could do!"

He finally reached me to issue me a certain street address. I nearly fainted. The precise detail, given in such a toneless voice, was weird—the hour, the number of floors, the street name, house number, which way to turn in the hallways to get to the apartment, on the outskirts of town.

I feel a need to give proper names to everything, and later I was to call our tryst spot "the slum," and, in my moments of anger and cold contempt, "the dump."

My heart was beating wildly, on the fourth floor, nine in the evening, August 10, 1983.

The measure of the ridiculousness of it all was my designer silk clothes, for this dump. The measure of my infamy: getting myself all ready to go stand before a man. It was everything I'd hoped for. He and I, alone, finally. And I was running the risk of all the things that can happen to any woman in cases like that... Being had, pure and simple. With all the dangers that implies and all the results it could have. Hadn't a relative predicted that certain women are black dahlias, the very seed of Evil? Referring to me, it would seem. Since turning down a moth-eaten or dishonest husband, or any bad match, was just plain bad. And the most intolerable is a woman who has choice but has made the wrong choice, an existence and drama that she can't even blame on others. They all look at her, shocked,

26

distrustful, disoriented and cowardly. The ugliest louse and the most spineless husband are a match in the view of the old bats whose breasts are bouncing off their knees and the patriarchs whose equipment has become goatskins full of fat, empty of what once gave them vigor.

The man was elegant. Which is to say that nothing happened. Except an unchained torrent of feeling. A kindness, and a caress, lasting two or three hours. When I left it was in a state near that of the gossamer delirium of love.

But this slum, as I called it in humorous moments, had a really sordid kind of ugliness. Anyone would have thought the place harbored the escapades of one or two men nearing old age.
For a woman whom art and beautiful objects had often rescued from her frequent bouts of suffering, really I should have fled after just a glimpse of this roach hole.

After two years I couldn't say in whose place I was coming to live through my many explosions. He's always denied that this was his property or had anything to do with him. Women today bring their lovers into their own homes, and more power to them, as they can escape the mildewy smell and dusty carpets of sordid love-nests maintained by so many rogues for their rendezvous, episodes of appalling and contemptible debauchery. Ugliness clings to man-and-woman moments, even in sumptuous palaces of white marble, the tombs of illusion, the grottos of shining certainty about pure maidens...

It's humiliating to experience your peak moments in random places, places of deceit.
That aside, I knew there were lots of women like me on earth: the ones who, for whatever reason, were cut off from

sex. Repressed and bruised, with mournful gaze and jawlines haggard even when overweight. The challenge of my relationship with this man seems to translate the general lack of interest I then had in sex. Seeing him so little, suffering so intensely from the feeling of love and lack, all that merely showed me the wall of cut stone there has always been between me and fully licensed pleasure, easy and easily repeated pleasure. But then I was ignorant of all that, as in those situations that are so bright that you can't see anything. You're dazzled by evidence that then disappears, as it doesn't fit the cruelty of the situation, the feeling of contusion, the appearance of soul wounds, of bruises darkening the skin on your defeated chest and arms.

The desire to make love stormed over me like an unfurling of uncontrollable forces. Very rare, very strong. One time it felt like a burning between my legs—I was waiting patiently in a car, R… Street, somewhere in the world under a gross and sullen sky.

A few months later a throbbing took hold of my stomach, in brilliant weather above a calm sea and a stretch of intensely green foliage: I was going down a network of paths like the meanderings pleasure takes to reach you.

A Man needed to come and be my ideal and idealized partner, the impotent partner of a walled-off woman.

I didn't know, arriving that tenth of August at the slum, what it was to have a lover—even less to have an affair. Prudery along with the complete elimination of sexual matters in my upbringing had eviscerated whatever erotic culture or basic knowledge might have entered my thoughts. I refuse sexuality with all my strength. But a dull need for its banquets had been slumbering at the base of my stomach, my fantasies and my reticences. The rectitude of the men and women who raised me had framed me in the body of a puppet or even a scarecrow, characters stuffed with bran, straw or old rags—their convictions. It had never occurred to me to rebel. They had succeeded perfectly in crushing what God had given me as strong desire and as the keys to reach for it. It's clear that happiness, like good luck, is built-in ahead of time, in the destinies of men and women. They had forbidden me to feel like a woman, to savor it at length and to catch a foretaste of paradise in the nest of a lover's arms.

Basic honesty signals that this adventure was special and unique: a single human life doesn't allow you to reach this height of intensity more than once.

We spent some marvelous times together, like the ones in fairytale endings and all the legends of great loves. I'd never heard of such wonders in the life I'd been leading; people were married, and the women spent the day recounting the vileness of the men they were going to share a bed with that very night. The only references for me, in my memory, were stories from books and movies.

Only scattered elements of happiness really got to me, out of those fleeting and textureless moments. I'll never know how it was for him because he doesn't love himself. And doesn't love me. When I say "I love him" I'm telling myself a tale, like that jejune literature that lets you borrow a dream, through scant words and images, books sold in train stations to a rough-hewn, pedestrian crowd. Still, Delly had nourished my absolute belief in a Prince Charming and his future appearance, his obligatory appearance, in the life of every girl. These readings, these insipid and inherently mediocre—even ugly—texts had constructed my phantasmagoria of a love, now converted into a permanent projection onto the future of our meeting, a projection just as impossible as those tales of shepherdesses and princes, princesses and shepherds that erase all the impossibilities, every impossibility that might arise in those false places, as false as the denture in the mouth of a horrible, toothless old man.

In his arms I was a woman, defeated, penetrated with sweetness and, in a word, unconscious beneath his kisses, the smoothness of his tongue, the calm his arms brought. But it was not really a genuine intimacy. The man was made in such a way that his need for tenderness was insatiable, but this delicious, courtly, tender connection—exaggeratedly tender—only lasted while our relations were mostly Platonic.

I should add that I was offered up, virginally, to caresses that could never satisfy my wild need for a true love. A great love. As rare as the Grail or the four-leaf clover of life's meadow—every dazzling discovery, we have to admit, being no more than repetition of a forgotten past.

I left there floating in the air, untouched by anything material, in a world where every kind of pain or suffering had been banished: I was in love. Utterly. It was pure splendor. The dusty streets looked to me like the shining rivers of Eden.

And then, a few days later, full of a doubt with foreshadowings of hemlock, I was hit with the disenchantment that old people feel: was I really in love again?... —People, ideas, books, places, impossible hopes...

Shortly before, talking about love with some friends, my face went so glum that the Consul asked what was wrong. I answered with what must have been confounding assuredness, but with all sincerity, that I was convinced I would never be in love again. He laughed through brilliant teeth:

"You don't really think that. You're an odalisque, and you'll author a great many ravages before you're done!"

The habit of confusing love with battles and massacres, putting women in the position of hetaeras or courtesans who thwart and flatten men, that way of talking said nothing to me. The only believable love is love for God, in mysticism, asceticism, and the life of hermits—the farthest thing possible from ordinary humans.

Still I was really hurting. It had been so many years since I had truly loved anyone. I even forgot to ask, really, what "odalisque" meant to him. I knew he was crazy about painting, and in painting odalisques abound—pink, paunchy, round and desirable in the painter's eye, but his own wife wasn't very odalisque, her sharp brown features more like those of a soldier on campaign.

As far as ravages go, I was more like the victim. I very quickly returned to the slum, all in raw silk, eyes made up and mouth soon to be wiped clean of its crimson. Just like that, with a kiss that toppled me, he removed my lipstick, inhaled the various head-spinning perfumes, and brought us to our knees, still kissing. That was the only prayer we ever made. Two primitive idols. Man and Woman, face to face.

I was weakening. He understood—down to the slightest one—my every shiver, and kept on. Then we talked. I'd have to admit I couldn't say what we talked about, at first. We had rivers of information to share. Were we really to enter into communication? And then, the matter of sex… It had been about sex from the first day.

Even that first time I saw him, when I was so exasperated by a blind hatred of everything he seemed to be. The inverse of the main feeling for him that was going to sweep over me, marbled by this same blaze of hatred. This hate suffocates me at times. It's so intense it seems to annihilate me. Realistically, he's not worthy of inspiring these feelings, of the emotion he triggers with no logic except the adaptability of the soul and the mind, and the impossibility of explaining their dance. But the tenderness I could offer him is blocked by his inability to be happy. So naturally I go back to hating him, to sharp moments of wishing him dead. I'd like him to

Chapter II

"She came to see me, and, though the perfume had not started to mix into her robes, her sleeves gave off the scent of musk!"

Al Motanabi

—Thus, speaking of one thing and another, we came around to talking seriously of desire. I was like all tormented beings, frightened and stalking the future. I dared, like Clitidias, for the first time—because in love the only losers are the ashamed. That phrase had hung around in my mind for ages before suddenly becoming clear. The problem announced itself with an extraordinary sharpness since, once again, I had no choice but to leave on a trip. Already having complete confidence in him, I had explained the realities of my needing to travel and he was convinced. It strikes me as intolerable to love without a perfect confidence in the loved one. I'm disillusioned of that, too, these days. People love each other in a circus of lies, an arena of deceit.

As for me, I was sadly divided by a choice that was impossible to resolve: give myself to him before my departure or postpone this moment until my return. The situation was more difficult for me than that of a virgin who's about to become a woman and is very scared. Because death is a companion always with me, my fear was that I'd run into it before making love to him.

Maybe I just wanted to become a woman, after all those years of making love surreptitiously, like a thief or a woman condemned to death! I had done so little of it in my life. I could cry now, and wish I could forget all that wasted time. Every second you gaze at in the life behind you is lost in the thickets of eternity, some great word, a yawning emptiness, and a tomorrow that will not come, the infinity ahead, days already buried.

We discussed it hurriedly, breathlessly, rationalizing without end. I was devastated. He advised me to leave, and we'd live "that business" afterwards. He knew I was going to meet someone. And he knew that my life was simple, legal and calmly ordinary—that the other way, the path of sin, was nearly impossible to imagine together with this path of decency.

Then, in the course of that same discussion, he confided that it was my presence and my company that delighted him the most. I was "very nice." A way of talking as pathetic as it was banal, a stream of mediocrity.

Beside myself, I sensed myself being resigned to the rank of especially ugly girls who bow before the prizes, bravos, and congratulations of an admiring jury.

My modulated singer's voice became colorless and stifled. So: I lacked all interest, all glamor, all femininity and seduction. It appeared that I could be secluded with a man three times in a row without his even trying to undress me. I was not beautiful. I was not a woman. No one could ever desire me. Not for a second did I ask myself if, there in front of me, there might be a tortuous and agonizing soul. Vague shreds of memories reminded me that he was a ladies' man and an inveterate and feared seducer. So I wasn't seductive? I had been deformed by my elders, my upbringing, the human bath of my scrawny childhood and repressed adolescence, brought up to think without reservation that man is my natural superior, crushing, and royal, because his organ reigns as lord over the universe which bows in its contemplation... I could only drop to one knee before this master, only too happy that he would deign to speak to me.

Again, I've insisted that it's slanderous to treat a woman like this—that, as far as I was concerned, I preferred to be desirable rather than bewitching or fascinating.

Between two lightning insights I made out a feeling that was growing in him, one he didn't want to kill by letting it burn up in our union. He was highly attuned to something emerging in himself—this love, perhaps unhoped for and miraculous.

He said nothing of this. He never told me anything to do with love. He doesn't love. But he had loved. Once, in a kind of gratitude because a woman had grabbed him up the way you seize prey or glittering objects of desire, showing him that he was highly lovable and desirable. Something he hadn't known, reduced as he'd been since childhood to not loving himself, and made weakly incapable of love.

This woman loved him wildly, I found this out through stories about her. He ruined her relations with her husband, and her femininity as well, because, finally leaving the intractability of the affair and this new man, she started heaving herself into bed with anyone who wanted her body. Or just about.

A year after the beginning of our affair, he disappeared for a week. On his reappearance, he told me "she" had come back, after her husband had forbidden her to come to our country. I was left speechless for a second by a passive jealousy so sharp that I clenched my fists.

And there had been another married woman—apparently he had loved her for eighteen years. That's all I could get out of him. He had a great deal of admiration for her.

I put two years into figuring out who this was, but I'm still not sure. I felt that if I could only understand why he'd loved these two women, it might be that he loved me too… One of those two was universally respected, but mainly because of much-admired her grandmother.

But really, I got to the point that I didn't suffer any more, thinking about that other woman, the one who was married. When it came to him, one suffering was replacing another.

If I had grasped, however little, why he didn't want to make love with me, "not yet," I would have left and never come back. It was some indiscernible and contradictory feeling that was drowning him...

I was about to freeze him forever in a posture of hostility, by practically forcing him to make love to me.

His "Right, let's get on it," lashed at me as soon as I heard it; his manhood, stung to the quick, couldn't retreat without diminishing. So it was my turn to want to step back. But the early ritual had started. I understood that he was intensely fearful of not being capable, such a moment of failure having probably happened a few times, or else far in his past. I helped him every way I could, with my scant know-how in this area. He had to teach me everything...

That first time has become blurred in my memory. It was hot. He was soon drenched. It was all kind of fast, I think. I no longer know. Did he undress me? In any case, he didn't put my clothes back on. I don't know if he even finished— this act I no longer recall. Communication died off. It was to be the body's creation, the body's finiteness. That's why so many have a smoke afterwards. Or just take off. Off toward other illusions, other desires still ahead, always the same, never satisfied and thus always reborn.

We had nothing more to say after. He was in a hurry to leave. I had lost my bearings. I stumbled in my disaster. I hadn't wanted this. I was still on a quest for ecstasies!

Instead, I was confronted with the body's evidence, it sad workings, the hatefulness of it. The mire and its regrets.

I had thrown myself into love-making with him for two reasons that wouldn't occur to me till two years had gone by. The first seems to have been to put myself to a test: we made love years after first seeing each other, years after speaking to one another, years after the time we took each other's measure like wild beasts who ineluctably must determine which is more fearsome, which will dominate. It was clear that, at his age, and with his importance, he had no more desire to love, and what I was was a "viper."

"A venomous serpent," which is proof of the enormous trouble men feel faced with women; they're afraid, they wait fearfully for the sting of a bite, and the poison, and death.

As for me, in a more real way, I wanted to help him get past this limping sense of his virility. He no longer wanted to fall in love, because in love he became crazy and emotionally very weak. He could no longer live diminished—his potency not tolerating the real proof of virility. The real proof, though, is bearing witness to the most extreme debility, man's presence in the face of death, a face his body bears him infallibly back to…

I've often thought of him as perhaps a homosexual. He never brought me any proof either way. He laughed every time it came up. The men who are closest to this state, those in danger of falling into it with raging passion, are the nastiest and most vindictive in denigrating it. Constantly on the defensive against this profound and gaping world within themselves, most often they elude the seducers, who fail to find them out and violate them, who would force them into the vigorous love-making of men, where it's about massive organs given over to a masquerade of love, elephants goring each other in a torrid jungle, their weaknesses setting upon them like horseflies and parasites.

The second reason, more solid or plausible but which could never have been assumed at the time, was that I suffered from some sort of inherent lack. Most likely he didn't want to stand in as an available lover whose job was to sponge away this deficit, a deficit wide as the world's great deserts. How can you know? Lack is the yardstick of the emptiness that devastates anyone who has a little extra courage—those who can recognize that life is nothing but a ridiculous parade whose figures are all dead, skeletons stalking about in carnival dresses and disguises of desirable flesh.

It was a failure on every level. I'd had a little pleasure without meaning to. He didn't seem right. There was no more talking. I lived one haunting thought, long as the tunnel of days that I crossed toward our future as a couple: *If only he wouldn't throw me aside like a dirty handkerchief you only use once...*

At night I left, alone, calling myself a low-life and imagining I was a lost woman with no safety net. I felt not only remorse but regrets. The wisest of women say this: "Grow old peddling your remorse but not regrets." They're right, but for that you'd need a soul steeped in life and totally without scruples, your every partner being no more than a road companion on the way to old age and the end, the final spasm of death.

He called the morning I left. He was kind and his calls had become absolutely vital for me. I spent an entire morning, from the far province I had reached, trying to call him. To at least have the sound of his voice.

The fat and resourceful woman whose house I was calling from didn't bother to rip me off as it was obvious that without this communication I was going to go mad. Her thought, instead, was to nourish me with fatty ham, a country loaf (sickly tan and not fully raised) and to slake my thirst with a warm beer we took turns drinking right from the bottle.

I came back, waited in a febrile state, hoping to see him again. No act, no possible step, no implication in the moves of my life seemed as essential as simply seeing him again.

Providence came to my aid, fixing him for two years in his professional life or in his preoccupations, without leaving him the chance to take off for more than one or two days. I took advantage of this twist, storming off myself after each drama, each doubt, each time a hint of dignity tried to pull me away from the love I had for him. My relapses were hellish. I struggled with myself as the drug addict with his syringe, the alcoholic with the edge of his glass, and with each episode I fell in deeper than the level I'd reached before.

As soon as I was offered the drug, the dose made me disgusted with both of us. My rebellions at the end of each encounter flattened me. And then the craving for him seized me once more, growing like a tidal wave; once again I swam in the opium of his presence. In the way of long-time gamblers, I threw the dice again and lost it all again.

Like all drug addicts, alcoholics, inveterate gamblers, pyromaniacs, and perverts, clearly I had sworn a thousand times that I wouldn't see him again, ever. I'd rather die. But life held no meaning apart from him. The conditions of the most sordid relapse inhered in the very vow never to see him again.

Then through an unhoped for chain of events, a party, a friend who was available, an autumn of lacerating beauty— the luminosity of that time of year is like no other—I ended up going the same way he was.

I'm a lousy observer, once I'm involved in a situation or a person. He was looking for me, in the plane, as if he were being hunted down. He didn't flush me out. I was so happy. He was once handsome. But that was already a long time ago. He's older now, and still very good- looking. His hair, almost white, is finer, and his fine waist is now less so. He can no longer look at himself in the mirror and fall in love with what he sees. He can barely say, "I'm old, and I'm still kind of good-looking…"

We went some place out of a dream, as the vulgar brochures and the fraternity of tourists would say. One of the most beautiful spots in the world? That could be, and I say this having seen a great many of the world's most beautiful spots. I've done them to the point of uneasiness. To the point of disgust. No place and no surroundings can reassure the attentive spectator about the passage of the clouds, the day, time itself. The passing of everything.

We got there by late afternoon. He had opened the window onto his balcony and was wildly looking out for me. Was he afraid I wasn't coming? A staggering happiness launched me into a kind of pool: the fullness of the moment was like that long-ago rest in the warm waters of my mother's stomach, when not a single worry obtained because I had not yet evaluated the horror to come, from leaving that nothingness. With my first cry I had understood that the air burns and that it was all going to be a tight game, lost in advance.

The giant curtain of his balcony floated in the evening breeze. The whole place seemed both blessed and privileged. And it was there that I knew the ultimate paroxysm. And what we call crazy love, in that expression both true and so false.

He saw me, came down to get me, and described how you find the place he'd chosen. In the same way as before. With an unimaginable precision. His lair was sumptuous—he'd understood that the fauna I'd become would take its rest there, finally at ease amid the pleasure of beautiful things.

Flowers. Fruit everywhere. An immense space. Rare landscape unlike any in the world, people came from all over the globe to see it: ochre, violet, vast and complete. It's true, there's perfection in the universe. Turning away from the windows I wandered among whites and blues, sinking into one soft chair or another. And then the four-poster bed, with carvings of two women profiled, arms uplifted in offering, doves on the tips of their fingers. Peace and femininity finally untied.

I was both cold and hot, my hair streaming, scented like a Salome. The potion we drank was thick, like the poison in a Renaissance prince's court, thus fatal. By the bed a collection of immortal poems. And beyond centuries, beyond all distance, Baudelaire, transcendent, his gaze despairing as it hovered over the beds of all the world's lovers, trying to express that it is but vanity and streams of illusion, this most magnificent moment—disfigured by death's magic.

There I lived my own death, and my resuscitation as well. Up till then we hadn't made love very often. I don't remember how we ended up on the bed. He served me. Welcomed me.

And I keenly felt his passion and sexual violence. I was marrying him, he was marrying me. That's what those moments were. They were magnificent nuptials, if marrying means going forth in adventure until a final fusion and a smile.

It wasn't until two years later that he told me we'd had the Wedding Suite. Before an angry God I will prostrate myself: *This is the spouse You predestined for me...*

He rode me with a precise fury and a bodily excess only matched by our quest for the dying gaze and the sweetness of our lips, the sweet tongue and saliva that became for me the most welcome of all drinks.

He took me in every position his fantasy could invent. I followed along with a talent I hadn't known I had. This was a moment of divine intensity. Like prayer in those lands, so far in the East, in Asia, where statues are raised to the erotic, where the goddesses' hips are the loin of the universe and the gods themselves are splendid creatures riding, astounded, on heaving female chests.

The rulers of the world were less powerful than I. Everything I had then read, the most striking works about love, now seemed literary mush, but Baudelaire's "*luxe, calme et volupté*" had finally risen to their proper magnitude and empire.

We didn't make love as if in sudden need, or even through pure bliss, and this was because of this moment's lack of real sharing—even when it might all come simultaneously between the most attentive partners.

One of them is always unsatisfied.

Shades of comparison, and also the impossibility of inhabiting the body and the true depth of the other. The moment of climax is a betrayal of love, meaning that we only feel our own and not that of the person we claim we love. We made love in order to haunt each other, to inhabit each other, to possess each other. I had never been so available to a man. As if I had never acknowledged a man's right to take over my body. Previously, as that sensation approached, I even felt disgust, or at least disillusionment; I went through a sort of refractory period—when I did give myself to someone—a feeling so strong that I couldn't even be near the man who thought he owned me—I preferred to get far away. I don't think you have to completely take over the other person—take, abandon, retake. All that is the illusion of a coupling that simply doesn't exist. It's a myth, or a dream—soon forgotten.

It never occurred to me to ask this man what was going on inside him. During the hours we were to live together I had to be right there the instant he felt the need of my presence or my body. I was spoken for, between a candlelight dinner and two lunches during which I laughed like a middle-schooler sneaking out with friends. I was happy in all my being: my body, my deeper breathing, my soft skin, other people, animals, the caress of the weather.

He locked me down the second he arrived. We lost ourselves in the madness of our beings, sometimes with no communication at all.

I'm fascinated by him today just as on that first day, when everything was said and consummated in our eyes; every gradation resides in him, those of sex and those of everything unreachable.

What I'm writing now is my latest attempt to conjure. "After this, what will I still be capable of?"

I could hear in my voice an offering of sonorous words, burning aromas, gilded stories and languorous tales of every imagined delight. He would listen, in devout silence. I could sense his bending, then regaining himself. Within me, unfathomable yet enjoyable movements took place. It certainly wasn't everyday life: The Man was uneasy with this disorder, these shiftings, this spirited sharing of inexorable Time.

The frosty nature of his temperament, his regal bearing, conceals only violence, exasperation, and incredibly strong desires.

I was to pay dearly for those incomparable hours. For two whole years he would take me, throw me aside, take me again. Shoot me at point-blank range. He would disappear— I would cease to live. At first, I couldn't even get him to reappear. He was going to "run silent, run deep," as he warned me…

Then one evening he called around midnight or one, with a simple "How's it going?" We talked for hours. My voice put him to sleep and I loved that—the motherless little boy he had been, finally cradled by a woman's voice lulling him to sleep. Sometimes he fell asleep so abruptly that his phone kept trying my number all night, dialing into the infinite, on his behalf, numbers that it struggled to reach.

43

So during the two years of this cursed affair (and it's not over) I read everything that all the world's literatures and every era's books have said, described, and repeated about Love. Everything. I learned some fragments by heart, from a recently deceased writer, torturing my mind in quest of his motives, whatever had dictated these texts to him. I went back to the eighth century in company of an exquisite Lady, who smiled—in an atmosphere of extreme refinement, far off, in the farthest Middle East—at her radiant Prince. And mine?

I would have liked to master every available idiom, to decipher the hidden meaning of all the mysteries that unravel in translations. I spent hours trying to delineate the difference between obscene, pornographic, erotic, and hedonist. And I kept coming back, without respite or recourse, to my passion. Yet nothing could cure my leprosy or soothe either my fevers or my inner enjoyment.

He was simple, hedonistic, erotic, pornographic, obscene, but never vulgar. I'm so grateful for this—with the result that I've never been able to attach myself to anyone else, in my miserable attempts to pull myself free of this spiral into the abyss, this spiral that's going to cost me so much.

I tried a few times to grasp the real nature of the feelings that tied me to this man. The matter was undefinable and impenetrable. Love is an undertaking for two. In my case it was more personal and unique since he...—didn't love me. My abortive attempts to escape him brought me back to a tighter bondage, devoured alive by my obsession with him. He's nothing but a wretch upgraded to emperor and magus—by the vital importance of my love for him.

He was indispensable to me, he still is, like light, air, and sun. At the mid-point of our affair, we set off again for that pink-colored house; it became one of the worst fiascos of my life.

He was sick, detestable, distant. He abandoned me coldly and with anger. I showed my disappointment. And we came to blows, striking out savagely on the bed like pariah dogs. Slaps rang out. Each of us gave and received, one-upping each other in physical pain, humiliation, rage and extravagance, in the pleasure of excess. Our faces burned. A conflagration of hate took over my chest, I who am normally devastated by aggression.

After this stinging disaster I erased that place from the map. The night before leaving I hadn't slept (our visits lasted twenty-eight to thirty-five hours) because I had begged him to sleep with me and he had turned me down brutally. I could have killed him. I waited for daylight. I was a mess at the airport, fatigue and sadness pulsing in my temples. Nearing our arrival, the plane had to circle because of fog; I could see it in fat, opaque banners, making a nurturing bed. He, in the same row, but across the aisle, didn't move. I moved through a hollow, a slough of anguish. Basically, what was wrong with death? Planes really have no business in the air, once they're up and away. Here was a Monday morning I could have used otherwise. We were among the first to deplane, and he was suddenly surprised, stepped aside to let me pass. He had completely forgotten my existence.

I wasn't expected to see him for days and days. If the slightest thing came up he would disappear, which left me in painful suspense, wondering if it was all over...

Then the loss of a relative gave him more reasons to disappear. When we saw each other again I was dressed all in black, very studied, very obvious. My make-up was much lighter than usual. What I was trying to show was that I felt his pain. That it was unbearable to me that anything bad should ever happen to him. He paid not the slightest attention. The funeral had worn him out, because the distance was long and people had eaten and drunk a good deal. He'd received innumerable condolences, the expressions of grief due to the great and powerful when they lose someone.

I was stunned. His relative was so close to him—I could picture myself in the same situation, crushed by grief. He was gray, as always, having been working but, in addition, having "had a lot of work to do," a formula he often used and probably the truth.

Frankly, it was chaos for me. I too had met him in order to condole. And it wouldn't come out. Console him a bit? He had absolutely no desire nor need for it, and it showed. On top of that, we made love. I left, wobbling without compass.

What was this guy, a monster? A loon and a monster? A degenerate—one I continued to love. Living these moments I often thought of that horrible figure, in a novel, and of the woman so taken by this man, her dubious alcoholic. I was as out of my depth, as pitiable, as the poor woman in *Le Repos du Guerrier*. But my guy didn't drink, didn't smoke, and pounced on me as soon as we were at the slum, those times when he could make it. His style was to hurl himself at me, as if overflowing with his own feelings or my lack, as soon as I swept through the door like a hurricane. Which was only an exercise in style on my part, since it was always open when he was there—lying in wait, motionless in the silence.

On the other hand, I had a way of advancing toward him as one does toward idols, gods, and holy texts. But in both cases a stiffening—first in one of us, then conducted to the other, in fractions of an instant—brought on hesitation and disappointment.

Often I left empty-handed, after the stench of the hallway and the rows of sordid apartment buildings I could see from the top floor: he hadn't shown up. The diapers drying on a balcony across the way suddenly seemed pointless, ridiculous; so a woman had actually let a man stick her with a baby?

And then I would go through unbelievably tough times. Clearly—had I no more importance for him than my old suitcases or my oldest shoes had for me?

Love often left me gasping, and I was like a dislocated doll in his hands. But whenever he opened his arms I fell still further. I'd have given everything up, abjured everything, if he'd asked. My Father, my Mother. The two of us were lawless and faithless, after all; perhaps we had no more Father or Mother. He was my Father and I was his Mother... The body argued my case for me; he adored mine. Maybe it was because of this that he had not completely disappeared.

In our love we reached unique summits and passages. Especially when, during those moments, we started talking. At first it was hardly real—in several languages, beyond the one he knows but I don't, and those I could have used but he doesn't understand. Love's language, however, is the one that surfaces in the eye's soul and in the soul's eye. To speak Love is to destroy it; to live it is to wear it down, sully it. Pulling back from it is the only way to find your way back to it.

In those moments it's not stimulation that swells, nor the abject lure of pornography. It's love's truth-will-out. As soon as this little custom took over with us—talking while making love became indispensable—the affair started to seem the focal point of any interest I had in the world, and, for him, it became a unique way of getting close to a fabulous partner (because, instinctively, I'd brought on such a montage of sensations that my embrace was indelible).

I lived, as a person, only for those instants, none of them easily gained, when I would be on top of him, under him, melding us together like vines in the primeval forest. You could only pry them apart by breaking them. Whether real or false, these are the only moments of generosity, when he is somehow my husband, thus also my relative…

The music of words (words awkwardly said, gauche even, and gauche because they're said) can cradle in anyone that distress felt deep inside, distress that can never abandon its solitude. When two people leave each other, just after being joined together, the illusion of this cradling soon fades, a fleeting dizziness, as brief as the joining of bodies.

I understand why I used my voice in a certain way with this man. And my skin and my lips and the perfumes and changing scents of my body. My hands slapped, yes, but also offered the greatest of tendernesses. I kissed his eyelids with the devotion due to gods. Slowly I brushed my tongue over his eyelashes and eyebrows, a little like a cat licking its young, tirelessly and with no feelings of disgust. He gave in to it all. The moans of ecstasy that came from him drove me on to the very well-springs of his pleasure. He got me used to a new, incredible boldness, incredible in the rigid woman I'd been until I met him: I now prefaced every love-making with the most knowing caresses.

And then I was swept with waves of desire. I savored his being with a voluptuousness that grew more assured and more convinced with every meeting. I would never have accepted all that from another man. The disgust that used to well up in me had completely disappeared with my lover. And from fairly rudimentary ways, in my sexuality, I progressed toward a triumphant confidence in my femininity. This ailing man, handicapped in his virility, had created a full and absolute woman out of the blocked and limited person I was before. It's my wonderment about this phenomenon, and my happiness with my new womanhood, that attaches me to him like the figure nailed to the cross. I feel that I could never experience this plenitude with anyone else. Yes these emotions and these convictions are only a trap. There is none of this, really, in what we share. I became a woman thanks to my own will and sincerity—the protected islands—of my own femininity. He foundered on my reefs and now I think I have stretched him on my couch. Totally untrue. He is in the shipwreck of his own infirmities and his incapacity to give himself body and soul. His belief is that no man should ever yield himself nor wallow in the precarious state of that gift:

"Take me as I am
I want to belong to you only"

He intimated the command to take him in my mouth—that or I would lose everything else. For the sake of form, I made it seem that I wanted the same thing. He allowed me this pleasure now and again, when it pleased him to. But I was clearly not to expect the same gift from him. I became very expert. His desire grew so strong that he would throw me on my back, charge into me like a maniac, moaning and opening me with no trace of delicacy.

Sometimes his sweetness swamped me like the dying day's light veiling a weary earth with gold.

At times I would pass out under him, which panicked him. He sometimes said, "We have all the time in the world," because my haste seemed to him a fear of losing it all. He had various ways of reassuring me—that our togetherness was not to be short-lived.

I was his mistress. He was my lover. There was not a soul who knew about us.

One thing about him left me wondering. At all costs he had to bring me to completion, even if he were to die trying. In summer his whole body swam in sweat and fat drops fell from his forehead onto my face. He gasped, choked, and labored on, and the more my pleasure delayed the more he increased his moving on me, to the last spasm of strength. Even as he failed, he continued working at me, as if I must one day regale posterity on his behalf, and his glamor wouldn't suffer from it. This always moved me a great deal, usually to tears, and sometimes I faked my pleasure for fear of exhausting or hurting him. And that's a way of saying I loved him—*I* did, the one who is also fully capable of assassinating him if it were possible to get away with it. That's not the whole truth; I would gladly be his wife. Or at least the woman to soothe his troubles and hold his hand as it slackened its grip, on the doorstep of sleep, or of death.

I used to show up at our rendezvous like pleasure's professional—a professional of refinement and indulgence: my body was cared for with obsessive research; the guiding principle was to achieve a regal elegance.

All the time women waste getting ready to see the beloved again could be time added to eternity, and could at the same time confirm that God is Beautiful and loves beauty. If those were the conditions, how could His creatures *not* be struck by His divine beauty and not try to devote themselves to contemplating Him from within their speck of human beauty—a beauty He created?

I gave myself over to this new pastime the way you bring someone a package containing a gift of enormous value. Silk, watered silks, linen, beiges and whites of every shade, splashes of clear water offered to myself like pearls, underwear befitting a queen or a perverse teenager, silk stockings or stockings of shocking colors, periwinkle and madder, for example, the rarest scents in the world—bitterness forgotten, my heart in a trance.

He would welcome me with his gaze, never kissing me, would hold me against him, squeeze me. I would shatter myself against the ice field, after having botched my professional work, rudely dismissed someone, after being crude with one person and terrifying with another.

Not one of these refinements interested him. He never had a compliment or any sort of admiration for the effort I put into my appearance, effort I knew to be frenetic and extreme—even for certain effects that were the height of inventiveness and marvels of human ingenuity. His curiosity only went as far, now and again, as asking about a clouded blue effect I'd achieved, or the origin of some extraordinarily exotic punctuation. That was it.

One day I nearly fled when he showed up unannounced at ten to noon, knowing that I left a beauty parlor then.

Flat shoes and bulky wool clothes, face unadorned, hair wet—I blanched with indignation.

He had flushed me out at my plainest!... We stood there in a stir of feelings, sweet but also raw. He had dropped everything to come see me or surprise me or spy on me or check the truth of what I'd always told him. Or perhaps because the desire to see me was irrepressible, impossible to put off. I was touched as I always was when I saw him, and a long pause reigned before I could regain my composure. I was furious to be seen with my face like that. I was tempted to think he loved me. It's probably that when you're a very busy person there's not an hour to lose to dash a good distance just to catch sight of someone for a few minutes. Sure enough, we saw each other for just a moment, a glance, a smile, a few words, and the short steps to our cars.

Another habit soon developed. When he followed me, by day or by night, in his car, we looked very intensely in each other's eyes for exactly one second, that second in which we disappeared for each other. This gaze formed just as our paths diverged, cruel proof that we could never collapse together at the end of a hard day or catch up with time's too-rapid flight. In our lives, too full, ill-crammed in fact, we succeeded against all odds in tearing a few moments free. If only our fates had been aligned, our human weaknesses would surely have been overcome!

He called me to his house and we made love a few times in his immense bed—a bed so big it allows you to sleep alone in your rocky marriage. I was jubilant, because I was now going to be a memory for him, ever present at his instant of falling asleep or awakening.

We made love there with absolute conviction. When this man touched me I became air and fire, sparks and flames, in the murmur of a rising tide. I felt something, and if I'm wrong (I don't think so), I'm only fooling myself. I've only been really alive and present in the world when in his arms. My life has flowed only in those flashes, clinging to his smooth chest, his ravaged stomach and the slenderness of his body.

I had no other sparks or dazzlements. The man I knew fooled me. For him, it's so clear: we make love now and again, and that's that.

And—I foresee it all—after him it will be the end of me. It's not possible that I might enunciate once more, or write anew, concerning another man or *for* another man, this whole magma that has swallowed me. It's as clear as death putting an end to life.

One mustn't believe assertions like that. A couple is only an absurd struggle against the sadness of finiteness and death, and the defeat of the latter, for an instant, in the warmth of a hand, of a whisper; it's proof of life pushing through your veins and pulsing at your temples.

My rebellions were so fierce that he took off for weeks. To punish me and to no longer be afraid. I screamed at him, like an unleashed fury, like a wild beast mortally wounded:
> "I'll never give my body
> To any other jerk!
> If I keep on giving it to you
> It's because you know it so well."

Only rare moments of serenity have been granted to me since this affair began. I've dedicated them to reflecting on the nature of the strange ties that bind me so violently to him.

I've already realized that he was my Father and that I was his Mother. But I'm filled with him and intoxicated by him, day and night. I'm connected to him, whether I'm stretched out naked, doing what he wants, soaring above the Ocean, out beyond various countries, buying flowers, or watching the moon and its evolutions. He is my kingdom and my collapse. He is my lord and my truth. He's only a human being like me, a person in passing, but defined by this passage, a clink among the links of infinity and the chains of eternity. Both of us, Man and Woman, think passion's torrents are somehow an effective weapon against nothingness and the absurd. We're both immeasurably small, and should never have left the Garden of Eden. There, God watching over us, none of these crazy sufferings could have happened—of which the main one, the most searing and virulent is the pain of love.

Why am I in it, then? What derelict future am I steering toward, with no guardrails?

Sometimes we had to change meeting spots, one bed or another being already occupied. That was tough in winter— both of us cursed these moments—after breaking in a concierge (not always that friendly), to find ourselves in a random bed. Appearances actually helped; I didn't look like a whore. These new places awakened an animal curiosity in me, my nostrils flaring in unknown territory. I checked everything systematically and criticized every nook and corner, because I wanted a house, a house of our own...— something he pretended not to understand. Chance loves like this are infinitely more common than many salt-of-the-earth people think. They give us the courage to bear the ineluctable slide towards the dancing kite of death.

He had me, even covered in blood. We washed the towels and, so that things didn't get any more complicated, I told him we could just bag them and throw them away. My arrogance and ability to improvise as we went along astound me even today. Basically, I've never loved anyone, including any man. He's the first one I love, in defiance of all these debaucheries. And I love him only because he's restive and withdrawn, leaving me some hope that the breaking dyke of his feelings might drown me in a tidal wave of that mad, redemptive love—a miracle in the long desert of days...

One day I followed him, abruptly, without any cards or ID, bags and pockets stuffed with cash, grabbing any plane, of course, and running the risk of hotels with no room. He doesn't know the slightest bit of what I go through to survive, to follow him, to accept his draconian conditions.

And paradoxically, all the other important things in my life—they're not getting done. What's going to happen to me?

This is what's called having someone under your skin? For me, it's more like having him in my brain, my viscera, my eyes, all my senses, and yes, my skin...

He should make me his queen, an idol mounted on a shrine, a zephyr to his tranquil mornings.

Instead of that, he makes me repeat, in the throes of passion, I'm "Yours... Only yours"
and "Yours... I'm all yours!" There you have it. A go-wherever at his personal disposal. Poor man, mad and depraved, who was never able to believe in the splendor of a woman who loves!

But he's unfamiliar with this nomenclature. He knows what a whore is. This man who never once said a filthy word in front of me. And there's my youth. My opportunities to live some other life. Massive waste in the waning of time that leaves women hump-backed and men fat, with an apron of rancid fat around waists which were once, just yesterday, vigor's own loin-cloth below their stomachs.

A funereal dejection hits me when I need to see him and it doesn't happen. At those times I have to drag through bleak and meaningless hours to pull myself out of it, hours long as famine and desperate as all human fate.

One evening he came almost out of duty, then suggested what sounded like a quickie, as he had to rush to a dinner or some society event of that kind. Bitterness and anger flooded my eyes. This was one more blow. Suddenly I couldn't take it. I asked for a handkerchief. By the time he'd come back I had slammed the door. He'd seen me crying and I detest crying, though I've spent hours, days too, at this somber occupation. Women weep and it makes them beautiful, they say—an absurdity, and utterly false.

Still, I am at an age, as a woman, where there are no more surprises. All we can do is use up—in the moment, in the flight of the days—whatever existence brings for us. We know the depths of our bodies, the extent of our needs, the tightness of our boundaries. The dice are cast and, the cup being full, we have to drink. Nothing really unpredictable will happen because we repeat, both men and women, the same old behaviors again and again, like animals stored in cages. Life is a cage and we scrape our skin at its fringes, with no let-up and no mercy until the final act.

My Mother having taught me nothing, along with my gleaning of nothing but the fantastic, I spent the next twenty years after my dislocated adolescence trying to get back on my feet. I still haven't got there. To telescope this long story, My Mother and this man have been thoroughly harmful for me; the ones who should have given me life, and then given my existence polish, could only lead me in the winding paths of suffering. I wonder, then, why go on with the whole process? Well, don't we all just trundle after death's process?

Don't we all just heed some "go" signal, and then unfailingly stumble along in footprints already laid out?

Shores I've yet to see—for a woman, I have a lively curiosity; I look much younger than my age, my profile is like a teenager's, and I often feel I've been saved from desires, and from some of my abilities and bolder ideas. I'm a very young woman, for having never lived. And the young lover with great, dead eyes, himself dead from having never lived their love, that's me as well—spoken as well as embraced by the masculine, in a clash of two unsound virilities.

I side-stepped certain orgies organized by women, having no gay feelings. Certain dawns found me leaving on my own, after nauseating parties watching the human cattle-show, their drinking and drugs all the while groping like the blind and staring like haggard monsters. In that spellbound place facts took on a bizarre meaning, discordant, impossible to believe. People sought out only the debauched, and aspired only to orgasm? Women kissed other women, joints were passed, and intoxication was already sloshing in every eye. Wildness reigned in the silences of some and in the gaze of others—lusting and half-drowned. The men wandered from living room to bedroom, checked out what was developing, made their choices among the most ready prey, the most alluring. I left, both sickened and stupefied. What was I doing there? Who was lost, who was heading astray, precisely, during those nights? Could you lose yourself that quickly, between the dark and sudden dawn? I walked through the night's last blackness. And magic happened. Horsemen were returning, filing below the old walls. Their costumes were magnificent, flowing with white veils. The horses were bays, with the longest tails imaginable. Some were very light in color, and their manes resembled the thick blond tresses of the sirens you see in children's books. It was a dream. I walked along, muffled in a cloak of violet wool. I was not afraid; the horses' hoofs didn't change their rhythm. It made an impressive song, or rather a splendid sound that echoed the depths of the night. I was alone. And victorious over luxury, wallowing, and debauchery. No one had managed to hold onto me, no woman had been able to convince me of time passing so fast that we had to create a rip in it—by my falling into her arms. They all had the same hideous and human project in mind, avid and overpowering—to copulate that night—simply because it had been arranged with just that intention, and because time escaped break-neck fast, and morning was looming at the end of this madness of drink and smoke, these necessary companions of partiers and lost souls.

Night in this city is a fairy world unique in the universe: at the edge of the known, the sky has the clarity of a child's gaze, and the stars are a child's eyes, candid and wide with wonder. A contrast in purity—with man's world, depraved by man's rheumy desires.

That place kept me awake. Having returned in the glow of its forgiveness to live there with that man, what I found there was no longer my disgust—but only that injustice which makes mortals of us all.

Several times, at intervals in that place's long night, I watched him sleeping, calm, quiet, as if dead. His discretion throughout life was like his sleep. His cleverness still looked incisive and didn't even seem to soften as he slept; I fled, half-dressed, gathering up books and jewels, to run off to the desired distance and bequeath him, on awakening, my absence. One of the hardest things to do is to sleep next to someone, because it's never an innocent process. Sleep is a pitiless revealer of people. You can get to the bottom of someone merely by seeing him asleep. A person sleeping is perhaps a bit frightening? Or ugly? If not, why are there so few subjects painted asleep? And no more are depicted sleeping, for that matter, than dead… This man felt no need to keep his woman's body next to him, in the sweet ceremony of sleeping together; he lived a complete affective autarky, as if he hadn't himself come from a man and a woman, but had been his own product.

That's why my heart started beating painfully against my chest when, one day, he told me how he was sweet and tender and affectionate when he was in love. All that, offered to another woman, signaled with the cruelty of a dagger in the flesh that he didn't love me; an extra confirmation, and I bled like a sacrificial animal.

The next day, I found him even more distant—a broken little smile, reticences.

It was useless trying to flee, I could no longer do that; it was a break-down in behavior, for me. Up till then flight had done remarkably, as a protector from others.

At those rare times I could be still, without trying to get some news of him, some impeccable reason, surging out of my despair, still made me cling to his memory like an octopus stuck on its prey.

But the prey always escaped, and my tentacles hung useless for days and weeks.

He disappeared—"I'm going deep," he warned—for two months. I thought it was all over. I went walking like those war widows whose young husbands have been torn away in a flash. A certain song played, drilled without rest, in my head. The voice of the tortured singer was searching the morning breeze for his loved one's murmur, as she came back over the hills.

I hid my acrimony and rancor when he called once again.

Chapter III

As time went along, I searched for the cause of my remaining ties to him. I had the sensation of loving him infinitely less. And curiously, at times, not at all. I regained, then, equal distance from all men, having no weakness, no hook for them on my soul or body—the amazon of every victory, laughing at all these males suspended in her enchantment and her varied fascinations.

Unfortunately, this state evaporated very quickly and everything returned to square one because, weighing everything, the joys this man brought me erased the weight of everything else.

Expounding like this on the suffering of loving him invokes little more than my meager ability to take charge of my destiny; I struggle to get up out of a puddle, then a few steps later I collapse into the same birdlime.

It looks as though this adventure is more like an affair for him than a love that might effect any bend at all in his trajectory. Hasn't he very clearly—and often—pointed out that we aren't even lovers, as if to be real lovers you have to be recognized as such by others?

If that first time I basically ordered him to accept my idea of making love right then, and not some other time of his ordaining, it was really to reassure him and soothe him about himself. He might not be as rigid and as strong as he tries—by every means possible—to appear. I was running the risk, that first time, of seeing myself thrown aside like dinner scraps.

If that had happened, I would never have gotten over it; I would have come up with a definitive lie, paralleled by the lack of conviction my body gave me and my resulting scant importance, my status as a woman of my age, my condition, my smiles, and my vanity.

So many men have scathed women with, "When I'm finished, I have no desire to see her anymore." Or: "She's OK for a roll."

"Women are objects…"

I shared my intense fear in those early moments that followed the first time, once our sexual couple had been more or less established. He didn't reassure me, appearing instead annoyed, or amused, or both.

My fear was my concern with attaching him to me forever, and having led him back to me like a horse to the plough was the proof of his accepting this.

When he made love to me, everything suggested that, without me, this man would be tomorrowless flotsam, and that I was as necessary to him as water, bread, and air.

He stared intensely at me, squeezing my hands, wildly kissing my cheek, caressing my body, stopping me from covering it again, making sure that I wasn't barefoot when I went to splash water on my burning face. Wiping my stomach the way you touch a baby girl in that spot.

Then, when he was all done, another being switched with him, possessed by vengeance at finding the weaknesses that had given birth to this trembling body and softened face that I idolized the way a homosexual man adores himself in the other…

He undressed me quickly and systematically, while I dragged my feet trying to make up my mind, sensing that my resentments were going to make me refuse him my body. I would have liked, just like him, to get there with the same alacrity, looking him in the eyes and hurling my clothes aside like remnants, showing him my casualness and giving in to my pure sexual rage.

He undressed me not like a man in love but like a man in a hurry, no kisses, no touching. The way I would take care of some lingering business I wanted to be done with as fast as possible, to move on to other things.

So the loving touches and the sweetness that goes with them were only there because I strove to pour them forth, while I bit my tongue in disappointment, receiving none of them. The kisses felt skilled but not emotionally moved. He was skilled and I was moved.

He was obstinate, refusing my gestures of kindness and softness. It was cruel, because gentleness and softness are not really my thing. He was deeply frustrating, at times.

When he started to sweat like a convict at forced labor in a torrid, insect-infested back-water, I would make a move to wipe my hands across his forehead. Real devotion, but something he couldn't tolerate. He jerked his head aside and let my hands fall useless, while I felt like crying. Clouds of vague, contradictory feelings surged up to drown me.

In this downward spiral I hooked onto his hips. This move had, in time, become the usual thing, and sometimes he demanded it as his right.

It all took place as if my job were to climb a mountain of bronze, each time, just to conquer an inch of his territory. If I had the bad luck to let go for a second or give up, I wasn't allowed to give it another try.

No became no, the most definitive no.

Refusing to let me sponge off his brow—did that mean I was pushing him toward his frailty and impotence?

We went through a maddening period when he insisted on proving to me, mathematically (a field where he's totally confident) that I could have any man and that he couldn't understand why I clung desperately to him. He explained me

61

to myself. He took pleasure—gently, patiently—in demonstrating how I was literally fantasizing him as something he was not; he claimed to have zero importance, no flame or even spark of interest. How he added up to nothing, and how my pious vow to see a mythic animal in him, a sphinx and one of the wonders of all time, was ridiculous.

The contortions I went through to prove the opposite didn't affect him. Every time this came up we had our fifteen minutes of sad-sack performance. And then I stopped trying to demonstrate the opposite to him. Instead I affirmed, ceaselessly, without respite, that it was my problem. Whatever was to hit me after this, he was what he was, that's the way things were, and that was that.

And besides, he tossed me. Into the arms of a friend, and in a very direct way, by means of a dinner. I had accepted, very curious that he'd wanted to introduce me to one of his friends to me who was, so he thought, a much better match for me than he was. He wanted to deliver me, bound hands and feet, to a certain monsieur of incalculable qualities: a tall look, great energy, exquisite musical erudition, a man very passionate and given to loving, remarkably sensitive as well.

I set off—yet again—towards the rendezvous, dressed like a dignified old lady, all in velvet—brown, ochre, and black, but intentionally exaggerated.

I steered through the evening, my head feverish with questions. But, why? My conclusions were all true, and not lacking objectivity. Unconsciously to put a friend of his to the test? To offer a very close friend the tastiest bite—or else a cast-off? To get rid of a woman who'd become demanding and cramped his style? I will never know the real motive for this act of his...

The evening was long and spirited. The gambit was men's business. I emerged pretty much unscathed, because, since the cradle, I've carried myself like a married chaperone. Not everyone is made for the gutter. It's in the genes, the environment, the individual.

Dinner was polite and enjoyable. These were gentlemen who had picked up the art of paying the tab, but you still sensed a kind of mining, a lack of that total ease which, when it exists, makes every moment pleasant.

I was amazed to see how discreet my lover was in this area. He belongs to that group that manipulates the rest of us, and to that end manipulators never reveal anything about themselves. They barely manage to maintain this legend about themselves, their poor selves, martyrs to their jobs...

I was struck by their manner with each other. The friend was touchingly considerate both with him and with me. In other circumstances I might have laughed out loud at the way they billed and cooed together.

They liked each other very much, you could see that. I didn't want to—nor could I—become some unhealthy bit of business between them—so I started recounting how my lover and I had met. And now I picked up on both jealousy and uptightness in the air. While courteous with the stranger, I spoke to my lover as if I saw him every day. I danced with his friend. My lover was steaming mad without quite realizing it; cruel, without mincing words, he burst out laughing, saying I danced the way you comb a giraffe. Both badly and absurdly...

I was close to slapping one or the other of them, or both. We drank a fair amount. Even my lover, who was usually as ascetic as a Buddhist monk. Then the friend started using the "*tu*" form with me. I really detest that brand of familiarity but, at the rate things were going, I accepted lots of things that didn't really matter.

And everything took yet another turn on the way back. My lover didn't disclaim his earlier attitude, far from it. He commandeered my car to leave me alone with his friend.

That had been decided completely against my will. I was profoundly irritated, as I never tolerate people doing what they want with me. The music didn't relax me; I was too much in love to find any charm at all in this new, overly kind man who hardly slept. I had no trouble raving, during the trip back, about my partner the torturer. And thus the affair of the new guy wrapped up quickly; his tact let him pick up on the intensity of my feelings for his friend. He didn't insist.

His name came up two or three times, then we didn't talk about him anymore.
"If you're not interested, I don't see why you're asking after him."
The two of them continued to call each other twice a day and to dream up all kinds of affairs and encounters.
Before this murky but incident-free evening we had just missed a chance at a threesome; the two of them arrived at a place just as I was leaving. My lover put the whole thing off, that time, by pretending not to know me.
It all had an air of a real three-way, and the feeling of masculine love. I don't think my heart is in voyeurism, or in being an accomplice, even if—with my passion for surnames—I had christened my lover's friend "ladylove…"

His way of dressing was very uneven, and he could go from jock hoodlum to lordly squire. What this caused in me was virile. I would have liked to kidnap him and make him my prisoner to serve my every pleasure. But I settled for contemplating his special distinction, composed of austerity and simplicity. He is handsome. His hair stayed dark until very recently and then whitened in just a few months, the way his face—whose permanent look was fatigue—picked up wrinkles just between two widely separated rendezvous. I noticed it when he was next to me. His face was deeply striated, and I choked up when I saw it. His aging was just like mine, that of the kind of people who don't age because their bodies remain very young, their desires exasperated, their joints not yet knobby, and their faculties intact.

Like me, he had traveled through years and years which, by all appearance, hadn't elapsed.

And this life, with its large blanks, had sculpted both of us like granite statues, because in order to survive we fossilized ourselves, we hardened, dwindled, and solidified.

When I'd seen him for the first time, twelve years ago, I should have noticed his sarcasm then, fixed his gaze and grappled with him.

His hands are twisted, as if broken, fleshless, dry and rough, with nails always trimmed but not really cared for. They don't probe, don't caress, but hurt when they strike and oblige me to do something I don't want to do.

His beliefs are rigid and monolithic. We speak a kind of mediating speech and, from time to time, I stop him because he's about to say "As you know…", as if we were in a press conference or administrative council, when only a minute before that we were crushing each other in a fiery duel, a display of eroticism and obscenity of every stripe.

He took up the habit of hunting me down in the places I frequent. Shamelessly, but still with his feline stealth.

We ran into each other "by chance" in front of large groups of different people without anything being possible between us. It was no longer feasible to not see each other in front of the rest; this lends an extraordinary dimension to everything that's shared intimately.

I would quickly terminate these false chance re-encounters whenever a server raised an eyebrow or a doorman turned away. I simply went elsewhere and he followed in my wake. One day, weary of my constant supplications, he said, "For heaven's sake, name the place and I'll come running…" A double-edged sword. He in turn asked me countless times to come to my house. At night, some holiday morning, for coffee, just to chat... I have always, still, refused with some verve. I don't know why. I would build him a palace and place its golden key at his feet...

For him, everything always has a mathematical simplicity. He constantly reproaches my complexity, my shades of meaning, my snobbism and my sailor's gross vocabulary.

The first time I told him
"I don't give a damn, you piece of shit,"
"I'm sick of this loveless fucking,"
I saw him writhe in his chair. And then... he started using a few of these words the way I did. So now he doesn't make love anymore, he "fucks," just like everyone else.

His cleanliness is really remarkable, he's ready to go to his maker at any moment, in an immaculate state of purity.

I used to inhale that smooth body, regularly shorn of any hair that was too long. A vague scent of cologne in his pubic hair made me smile—he'd had the thought that I would linger there. The fact is that I had drifted off while I was there...

We had learned parts of each other's obsessions, and mine had to do with deifying even the air the two of us breathed. I started burning sandalwood, joss sticks, bringing all kinds of accessories in to transform "the slum." Vials of perfume, shimmering clothes, indoor shoes. And even better, the slum had been done over, in butter, beiges, maroon, mauve, pinks, crimson, and off-whites. It had become, if not love's little isle, at least an average kind of place, not too ugly, that an interested woman could make fairly nice. The renovation happened because of a massive infestations of moths.

I was drifting between two seas, gaze fixed up above the bed, when I noticed some kind of larva or moth cocoon swinging from the ceiling. I knew the place was sketchy, but I still persisted in tasting the pleasures, and the tortures, of our affair because, after all, the sheets were regularly changed. And some of them were of really good cloth. I suspected The Lover of sneaking them home between his piles of fine linen and the more down-to-earth.

So I pointed out to him that fauna of all kinds infested the place, and that, despite the immense love I bore him, this was a bit hard, moths and cockroaches, not counting the sordid little office of the concierge, the elevators always being on the blink, and the pitiful ugliness of that whole neighborhood on the edge of factories, loading docks, crowded workshops, and dive bars.

I came close to being attacked, on leaving, one summer day toward the end of the afternoon. There's no doubt I was out of place in those environs. I used to show up like a boat with the breeze in its sails, like a whole garden full of orchids lofted on the wind, like a linden forest drooping with flowers.

Dressed in white lace, my hair wild, feet bare in sandals of fine, soft leather, I was heading for my car when six or eight young hoods—really rough-looking, evil, obviously stirred up and aggressive—arrived at my car just as I did. I calculated that if I tried to run I might not get out of it alive. I held the same pace. The most violent one jumped ahead, letting go a salvo of insults—raging like a madman. One of his buddies tried to restrain him, which drove him crazier. In the car, I let out the clutch, almost running over one of them. He slammed his hand on the trunk. I'd narrowly escaped; there was no one else around on that late afternoon charred by a hazy sun. What stays with me from that day is the alarming odor of trash cans, steaming in the sun, right near my car—and the certainty that I had escaped an atrocious fate. The howls of that young man still ring in my ears. Later, when I told X what had happened to me, he was his usual marble self.

As for that, in love matters he had the exact same bearing as the young hoodlum who wanted to attack me. Exactly the same. Virile, violent, vicious, inflexible, wanting to pierce a woman rather than ask her consent.

So he continued to claim the slum didn't belong to him, but it was after my discovery of the moths that it got re-done.

I saw him, in the slum, on the eve of one of my trips. I was quivering with excitement. This was during the hottest era of our affair. I was about to leave, and he offered that we absolutely had to make love. Which unfolded with fever, rage, madness, and somber death. Death was threatening us, clearly, and its incantation had to do with sex. The feeling of abandonment disappeared in our soaring skyward, then, suddenly, after the high point, a taste of ashes in the mouth. He left me behind, I left him behind. There was one beautiful moment of hope, the night before one of my departures. He called me from home, after getting back from the slum. Something I wasn't expecting. He asked how I was doing. My response was that a colossal doubt had taken hold of me, that I wasn't even sure I wanted to live. Guessing the profound suffering this separation caused me, he reminded me that I was the one going away. I said in that case he should be distressed, as I was about to abandon him. He seemed to agree:

"I think that's what I'm beginning to feel."

This was so unexpected that I let him off the hook, deeply moved, somewhat consoled, but beat up, and not daring to hold him to vows he couldn't make. And then—there was his reputation as a man without a single weakness.

Our hyper-sensitive delicacy made us switch topics, as our feelings had earlier been too wounded for us to risk overdrawing our balance of truth and affection. Missing him—his absence—oppresses me. My tears are almost beading up on my eyelashes. All I want is the freedom to be, and to one day escape this prison where I thrash about waiting for him.

I'm not sure how to make all this clear since even I don't understand myself. I have a philosophical, even metaphysical, sense of the most anodyne little things. When I see a parade of ants who kiss every time they bump into each other, I tear down and reconstruct a whole world. My thought escapes from the ant toward the animal Cosmos, so little understood by men, then toward the universality of appearing-living-dying, then toward the starriness of rocks, so marvelously available because they never die like plants, never abandon us. They are eternity before our eyes, and therefore reassuring.

My suffering when he leaves or doesn't call or won't say where he is is a stabbing pain. I felt the same pain when my stomach was operated on and when I had my tonsils out. Blinding, atrocious pain. You think you're not going to survive it. With my throat bleeding, I thought I was done for when they went to ablate the second tonsil. This is exactly what happens between one rendezvous where he doesn't show and the next, hoped for, where he may or may not come. My feeling is so strong that my life has no meaning without him. And what's more, the life he leads seems so much more transcendent than what I do and what I live. His life has so much more significance and impact.

Sometimes I tell myself that, though rare, beings as perfect as he is do walk the earth. But it's more a question of a special cohesion he has, and not the quality that others have attributed to him...

"...I love you passionately.
I would fashion incantations for you
And celebrate you
In your fabled uniqueness..."

What allows us to go on believing, haunted and mad, that the being we love is divine, without any paucity or stain?

Maybe, in our pitiful weakness, we conceive that all we can do without the Other is die, as if we were deprived of our mother. Blind little beings, hungry and half-asleep!

Step by step he has stolen into my depths, my uneasiness. I'd like to be delivered of him, and never love again. But what is certain is that as soon as I might be cured of him I'd be cured, too, of all the difficult and beautiful things about love. Our problems are all in the affective realm or else they don't exist—and we spend the greatest stretch of our lives coming to that realization. Alas!

> "My ambition is to offer you
> Calm mornings..."

You know, like that September morning when I started crying softly, just when we had to leave the pink city... You were leaving me for three weeks, and I knew it was three weeks' death for me.

"You don't need to be besieged by this obscene question—wanting to know the *why* of all this agitation, since in the end it's always the same..."

"My main concern is that you feel wonderful in every way, that you take pleasure in eating, drinking and looking at me, if you deign to do so."

The only real battle is with myself: to keep myself adorned, polished, perfumed, wrapped only for the benefit of my Master.

Which is to say that, whenever he's available, I will be his ecstatic bedside rug, his precious chamber pot, and the willing tooth glass where he surreptitiously dumps his second-hand bridgework.

I love you, Sir, in the hollow of your bed of prosperity, you who pretend to have so little, so smug that your poverty lives on beyond your chance possessions.

I adore you, Sir, thin, attenuated, settling. I live only for you, Sir, and your wretched body, your reluctant erections, your abhorrent pleasures.

I'm begging you, just deign to look my way, so that I can go on imagining everything I've dreamed of living at your side, things you want, too, but don't have the courage to try for.

Two centuries from now you won't even be ashes, and you will have lived like a coward, thinking only of what people will say...

Some future element, a speck in the spirit of the times, in towns by a future sea, will weep for your refusal to live and to give me life. Beating on the seaside ramparts where we were born, waves and crazed winds will howl from the deep—eternal litanies of our love, shattered by your inflexibility.

"We will no longer be,
Sir, anything but ideas hurled beyond the infinite—hoping to meet up again..."

Chapter IV

There came a moment when I actively struggled to break off the affair. He was no help at all. There were also moments when it all became even closer, became indispensable. Sometimes, when I hadn't seen him, I went to bed and stayed there. Until a last scrap of dignity goaded some energy into me.

I got to the point of issuing orders, and it happened that he obeyed.

For my part, the only time I ever missed a rendezvous was when I was stretched out on a bed in a clinic; I lay there calculating my strength, whether I could make it to see him. The fact is I could have made it, and collapsed in front of him, in physical shock. Or collapsed all by myself, if he didn't show up that day.

When he doesn't come, it's always the same few steps for me.

Five minutes of crazy hoping, with every possible rationalization. Maybe he couldn't find parking; he had extra work dumped on him, he'll come any second.

Then minutes tick by, become fifteen, become a half hour. And my sadness rises above me like a banner of mourning. My breathing goes weak, I double over, my hands and feet get cold—and I am ugly, as blood drains from my face leaving violet splotches on my nose. At that point my eyes have an unbearable sadness, like a beaten dog's, or like a child's, a child without parents.

There was only one exception. A day when he got the place wrong and came to see me at one of the spots where we often went. Clearly, I had waited enough—enough for him to remember, to start out again, to park, to show up! I was waiting. He was gorgeous.

Another time, I waited for him so we could go off together and spend the night. Not only did he not come at the agreed time, but he was brassy enough to drive right by where I was waiting. A few seconds after watching him go by, fast, with someone in the car, I had the idea of following him. But why? I'd seen that the other person was a man. And his destination wouldn't normally have taken him by where I was waiting.

Still, there were times when I imposed my will, and times when he bent. The whole thing made us war weary, both of us. One day I enjoined him to go to the city limits, to take me out to dinner in a nearby town. He imposed the condition that we go in separate cars. Which I found old-fashioned and pointless. He still wanted to follow in his car, but I parked and climbed into his. He was dressed all in white, right up to the white silk tie I had given him. I noticed the gesture and his elegance but kept silent.

We had a really good time, a second-rate orchestra, lots of tourists, and an overwhelmed maître d' who attended his every move the whole evening, servile in a nice way, even affable. They must have spoken before, reserving the table.

The food was nothing special and when they suggested some expensive alternatives, he didn't go for it. Annoyed by his lack of savoir faire, I ordered something else, to help him save face, without any awkward questions. Did he even get that? His cheapness is really unrivalled. He has never given me a flower, a bottle of perfume, or even a handkerchief—I who spend so much time crying. So how can I love a man who has so little generosity?

...Even if he covers me with perfumes from Grasse and Arabia, nard, and rose essence, the purest water and powders, embroidered towels and the dreamiest vesture, I will only be a ghost propped up in a white shroud, drifting like frozen breath over the tired earth...

However, that evening was delicious and even tender. I'd put up with any humiliation for a little tenderness—but can someone devoid of generosity be tender?

After the meal, we crossed through tropical gardens that reminded me of troubling times, places that belonged to the past. I pointed out the features of the trees' trunks, or their scent, things he didn't know. He retold the same memories for the thousandth time. His life seems to have crystallized around a very well-defined slice of his existence, but one that is irrevocably past.

I was so calm and so sweet that he embraced me under the giant trees. His kisses were much more enticing than usual, and I was as dizzy as if I'd inhaled the air of poisonous plants. His armor began to give way. He was finally beginning to live; he had never had an affair with anyone. I know that, too. An affair is the key attachment to real life and living, since without it something is lacking, even with a spouse, children, a home, and great achievements of all kinds.

We came back totally relaxed. I had almost thrown myself onto him, like an animal skin, my body undone by my feelings. He seemed happy, and tolerated my being draped on him—he who knows no touching that isn't sexual. He admits something, revealing to me that no woman has ever been in his car... Yet another thing from a century long gone...

On the way back I voice my whim to stop for coffee at a roadside spot. Partly to be able to leave him as late as possible and partly to prove my power over him. Of course, I was dressed as if for a coronation.

My long dress dragged over the dive's chairs. Nobody spoke to us. He remarked, very perceptively, that all the horrors of this bar, transplanted to Paris and barely altered, could serve as a meeting place of the elite.

We had this habit, changing palaces and also meeting like working class people in regular cafés. I adored those moments. We'd each park a little way off and arrive, under the trees, for coffee as black as sin and strong as my love for him.

Nobody but us could have pulled this off, and nobody else would have found any charm in it. It reminded us how far we had gone, the summit we had reached...

In those places I still disguised myself, at times, got up in any old dress, a throw-away, an almost colorless cloth. The fact is that I suited his fantasies, his hoodlum look, his regular guy look, by dressing up as a tomboy, a non-conformist, someone sure of her bearing and her views, and clearly owning the right to give herself this treat. Sometimes he arrived in a get-up that was a little too studied, but with his eyes hidden by dark glasses.

During a drawn-out meal, I piped up that I'd really like to come back there the following weekend. He showed up, when the time came, before me, and I saw him wobbling and craning among the tables, the people, the paths, the shrubs—in the fear, as I could see, that maybe it wasn't happening. But those were magnificent moments for me. It's always deeply moving, watching him when he's looking for me. And there was no doubt he was looking for me, unbalanced, out of his normal aplomb, barely hiding his agitation.

Often I was extremely late. When that happened, all he did was act a little huffy. It could never have been otherwise; he never raises his voice, always keeps his mood even, won't allow himself an outburst. Once, running late in the middle of the night—stuck at a deadly dinner party—I got myself rejected by him. He was wild with rage. I had misunderstood something. I tore my dress in frustration. But he made love to me...

Because I went back to him, shamefully, since I'm still not used to having a Lover. The afternoon ended fairly normally, and I invited him to have a bite in my room, because in these hotels we always got separate rooms.

We probably exchanged a whole bunch of generalities and inanities.

Then I found myself in bed again, with no idea how or why I'd followed him there. A good thing, because otherwise I was probably going to be bored. I was probably going to feel a familiar nausea, and disgust, because he really isn't all that amusing. Even in bed—which, let's admit it, is the real goal.

Then, suddenly, amid this low-key contentment, drama broke out.

He had been plowing away for a while when he commanded, imperiously, that I get on top. And me, well, even though I'd progressed through every stage of love, of the body, the bedroom, liberation with him, I found it difficult at times to simply obey his orders. I answered sharply, with a final "No," and "I don't want to."

Which bothered him more than you can imagine. Usually that's when we start hitting each other. He slaps me, I hit him back, hard, building in force, conviction. Sometimes I start screaming. That time, we reached new heights. Without backing down he threatened to leave. I didn't believe him. He did. He got up, got dressed with unbelievable speed and slammed the door behind him. I was a wreck. His repressed violence always devastated me. On top of that he'd openly threatened to leave for home.

I had to give in, after reflecting how sick I was of screwing everything up in my love life. I took off looking for him. I can still hear, as a condition of his turning around and coming back:

"And you'll do everything I tell you?"

Naturally, I did everything he said, and a lot more besides. He came back as fast as he'd left. Maybe that's all he wanted, the slightest sign from me, to change his mind? He undressed, got on top of me, forced me to take him in, stretched out on me, and, while pounding away furiously, said:

"In bed, I give the orders—understood?"

Something imperious, previously unknown and violently physical, sexual, made me almost die. I came to a second peak after trying every love move I knew. This was the beginning of the taming of this man, and, for every step that he conceded, he contested what had been yielded—for months, refusing to see me, for example, granting me absolutely nothing, not even a little time on the phone.

This adjustment to that incisive, masculine stipulation—*I am the master*—caused me to admit, definitively but not without difficulty, that even if he wasn't superior to me, still I had consecrated him as such—something he clearly loved and which was indispensable.

How can a woman derive pleasure from a man's insisting on his dominance? Aren't the most recalcitrant women also the most feminine? And what kind of woman am I,

78

shivering under a man who's capable of showing his preeminence with such ferocity?

But there you have it, that's how it is between him and me.

A particular phenomenon, more serious, and inexplicable, had arisen—and it bound me even more tightly to him—I no longer felt a moment of needy rebellion after intercourse. I could be panting right up to that moment, and, once the caresses were over, I felt only one need—to create some distance. What is not possible, on the other hand, is a fusion, a vanishing of the self into this union, thus replacing duality, the duality of the bodies, souls, sufferings—so much suffering, between those of man and those of woman, a whole universe, an abyss...

After this love-making, we got out of bed. Something was missing, something that might have brought a smile after delirium, after death, after thunder and rain, after the China Sea and love's own ocean. No, that was just one more session. And you'd have to use more painful terms—after coupling, or worse, after bedding.

We needed to get something to eat. And, calm as could be, he suggested going for seafood, since we were at the sea's edge. Triumph, for me! We were going public. No more of that obsession of hiding from everyone. Still, it was careless and crazy both for him and for me, considering all the social zones involved. Breaking the law felt great. This was one of the first times we risked ourselves out in the open. Like two very young people who just want to be together.

He sabotaged all my wardrobe choices. Even though I usually went around with everything you'd need to outfit a whole music-hall scene.

I got dressed agelessly, androgynously, in espadrilles. He was fine with the plonk they served us as if it were a fine vintage. I brought up, like a good soul, one of his favorite subjects, long-settled memories and rather stale ideas, and once again I savored his ease with life and living. In the end, he's very accommodating and kind, if only it weren't for that fearful ability to suddenly disappear.

He ate bread, lots of it, without offering any opinion on all the things we were offered. He might have been a likable travelling companion, easy and intelligently open to the world.

When we came back, it was back to bed, and we made love again.

There has only been one moment in my whole life when I am really alive: it's having him in me, and my being completely surrendered and consenting, and his being over me, as concerned for himself as for me. I called him Sire in those moments and he called me My Lady. He often demanded that I play the part of slave. I did this over and over, with no relief and also no faith in the role, without believing it in the slightest. The fact is that I made sacrifices to his banality; that was the price to pay in order to be with him. He needed to think he was more important than I, in pursuit of ends I can't imagine.

The specific quality of this affair—which made me lose control over the flow of time and events—is in essence passionate. Sprigs and whole armfuls of joy that I gathered up in my flesh, in a rainbow flowering of every joy I could have dared to try, or to hold back, ever since I've been of an age to desire anything. That is, for all eternity. And the ultimate distinction is that this conflagration could only have happened when our two beings came in contact—it's that my pain is truly great if he's not part of this cosmic movement along with me, a moment that soars beyond the impossible, a flash of light that mocks death and all the vanities. This twosome pursuing a chaos of the senses—

that's what has left me washed up, alone, on shores where this kind of paroxysmal frolicking is unknown. I caught a touch of his sexual obsession, and that has left me weak before other men. When this wickedness took hold of me, there existed only one possible remedy—more of him, and him alone. I can die calmly or in convulsions, it makes no difference. The slightest rain could sate the drought that reigns when he's stopped touching me. And yet, I was completely unsatisfied because he was so incapable of giving; he was weak, he didn't have the gift. He compensated for his weakness by the will for strength—which I confused with strength of character. These feelings and this passion badly borne and badly shared could never last in the profound absence of real pleasure.

A woman, a real woman, can't really give in to what seems like love if the man doesn't really fulfill her, in her intimate, innermost being, in her belly...

Healing water bubbles up in me from this pool of dews and liquids that he splashes over me and in me, replacing as he does so the cleansing bath of true love.

What tears me up is the fact that he loves me with body and sex, while I've lost my integrity and even my identity in this same passage that he's taken, yet I stray into real love—all by myself. There was a certain paralysis, when it came to really joining as one, and it firmly blocked us from calling each other by our first names. These two names were as taboo as God's, or as the most obscene name one can say. Twice in the throes of unbelievably violent emotions, as we rose to a climax, I gasped his name—all the while disgusted with my weakness, my lack of tact and restraint. He said my name when I urged him to, but giving it a slight twist. I was let down. Our backgrounds didn't overlap and thus there were limits in our already difficult communication. Yet all this was apparent only to me.

We fell asleep soon after that; he did first, and I followed, after a spell. It was the first time I was spending the entire night next to him in two years. This time he wasn't completely like the rigid wax doll he usually became when he slept. Our bodies wound together again. I had an impression of security—or eternity! I didn't feel like running away, gathering up my rags and trinkets as best I could. Sleeping next to him, that night, was sweet, serene, with the sea's faint murmur in the distance.

His unfathomable reserve made him wake up and quickly groom himself, like a cat scampering away on a terrace.

It's those faintly dubious moments that you go through— part of ordinary life. But something I wanted to escape. And he knew it.

We had always shown infinite discretion. He appreciated my ways, those of a fallen aristocrat; I could never have put up with an unshaven man, ill-kempt, hair mussed up. So he came back, had his first coffee. Then we set off on a long walk along the sea, still early in the morning. I felt so good that I began to see everything, and see it all with remarkable sharpness—the infinity of blues and greens in the ocean, the little ridges on the pebbles, the orderly flocks of birds, the fat gulls' gossip, the water pulled back so far at low tide that it seemed to have reached the horizon.

I noticed some magnificent vacation homes. Instantly I wanted to buy one. Or for him to buy one. So that I could enclose this story-book love within absolutely private walls, walls that cradled these moments, moments stolen from life and quickly over, before being really lived.

In spite of everything, he didn't give an inch. For him, it was just a stroll on the beach, without fever or romance. My fever was that of the sea, the bay's arc—precise as if drawn by an artist—the others ambling by and the few young people cavorting wildly. He was, it now seemed, simply a tranquil little father; his amazing abilities were only what I attributed to him.

A very sensible person—but not a poet. Not at all. He did have moments of terrifying emotion that he hid the way a miser hides his gold. I've heard him sob, a sob choked into a convulsion.

I've even caught him getting up before we were really done, hurrying to clean "all that" up.

I was cut off in the middle of a gesture, astounded that he wanted to control himself so much, even at times like that. What is this curse that frustrates him in the midst of the loveliest things, and cuts him off from the fearless happiness of ordinary people?

My plow-animal's patience led me, months later, to try to explain that sperm is sterile, just like urine or menstrual blood—that there was no basis, no need, to talk about being sullied by that kind of thing. He still made sure of this clinical cleanliness—even when he had me swallow his sperm the first time. The unlikely poetry that can attend matters of love could never further my quest for the absolute as long as he remained incredibly ordinary and down- to-earth.

I had recourse to extraordinary inventiveness; all he knew about women was platitudes and schemes, plain cooking and the everyday.

Strangely what he was expecting from my difficult and unruly orgasms was a jet of my own sperm. I wasn't all that happy that he'd always talk about my sperm while I had no burning desire but one—to be filled up with every offering possible from a single man, and above all to keep on being a woman.

Woman.

Was I more boy than woman, or was he more passive than virile? I imagine virility is tiring, if not exhausting. Having to eternally come up with erections must be physically wearying and inherently unbearable.

The complete man is a myth, at best a pious avowal and at worst one of the most insidious illusions ever invented by humanity. That's how I sense it, as a woman. I needed, then, a centaur and a priest, a poet or a warrior in Alexander's corps (in victory or defeat), or one following Hadrian or Sardanapalus. A mythical man—yet he was only somber reality.

My desire reached the point of wanting a child with him. Either as a result of the sensual loosening I was causing in him, or from the desire to be a mother felt by any woman in love, I often yearned to become pregnant by him. Then I was—and my courage failed me. The whole thing was insurmountable. Too many impossibilities. I gave it up.

Having your womb willingly filled with a child is, for a woman in love, a deep plentitude, especially in the middle term, before the child completely invades you.

Carrying this child is then the only concern and even the only justification in living, for the pregnant woman. Her dreaming and her mind keep coming back to this delicious load, this weighing down of half her body—giving her this rolling gait and this doubled swaying—the most wonderful love already replacing love for a man, that bestial and unclean love.

Nothing that flows from even the lightest of his touches is not marked with this immense, engulfing desire—a desire rising from the depths of me, to conceive a child with him.

The trap was irrevocably closing. In that sense, things are so constituted that everything must continue down a certain path...

...The real truth is that I feel I must create this child. Out of love, pleasure, and fascination. This imperious wanting arises—perhaps above all—because he's also ready, in all the ocean of impossibilities and death, to make this child. He is certainly moved, at his age, by the possibility, and by my desire, and by how marvelous this could be. In these moments a tenderness drowns us, a love that could never end.

This desire runs the risk of turning to awful regret when I'm no longer able to have children, unless, of course, I do this now with him. But from the other side of the looking glass, things are not really that way, perhaps...

Yet he showed me a few names for boys and girls. I often had a flash of intuition that this fruit of ours would be someone out of the ordinary, but that we—we would only be run-down and destructive parents.

Then, too, my doubts bore into me, my pessimism won out, and I resigned myself to accepting reality. Yes, I know you have to seize the things and the people you desire; nothing's ever granted or permanently owned.

This likelihood of our giving life to a new being grew steadily, because once this man was in me he no longer left.

What started to happen was that after making love he would stay on top of me for what seemed an infinite time; he needed this. I, in turn, was responsible for what I had tamed. I no longer recognized this man, fused with me, the man who had always jumped up to sterilize himself as if making love somehow gave rise to an unbearable stench.

I found myself dreaming about him, night after night, and woke up gloomy, with no enthusiasm for anything.

…One of the cruelest dreams seems to me to have a real nastiness, in the way it reveals what is happening inside him…

He was far off in another country and was trying to call me. There was a five-way relay, that is, five switchboard women, each one confiding the message to the next, and when the last one reached me, when she connected me to his voice, the line failed after he had said two words…

I felt pain during this dream, and felt as though I were suffocating. I was languishing, and could feel it even while asleep. I've already mentioned that we didn't call each other by our first names. One night, when I was especially strung out because I was leaving the next day, and despite having spent the whole afternoon with him, he came to me in my dream insistently begging:

"Call me by my first name"

And, paralyzed, I couldn't. I was about to leave for three weeks, to try to put distance and time between us. Without any chance of communicating. I couldn't do that either. I came back before I was supposed to.

I kept on struggling with myself, like someone cursed, and with this problem. Two years—that's a terribly long time, a painful and courageous length of time, to live through an obsession with a man who doesn't love you. It's like having a cancer in your soul because—even if you can go on living—some part of you gets removed and taken away.

I will never love again—it's not humanly possible for me, and only as a ruined, old woman will I survive this story of a love that didn't love me back. But not because he won't have loved me. I imagine that the day he says he loves me—am I so sure I can still hope for that?—I'll take a very long bath and go off to bed like an obedient child, half-smiling and half well-behaved.

If God only listened to me, I would pray hard, day and night, that he might grant me the indulgence of his love. If I were a monk, I would worship this God whose gaze is turned from me. If I were less lucid and skeptical, I would have consulted fortune-tellers far and wide and the sorcerers of secret societies.

… He is my love but also what sanity I have—I love him in me and he loves me in him. As for anything else, the day he tells me he loves me, I won't believe him. Do you believe a recidivist who repents, or a Don Juan now tied to one woman, or a hit man between two murders?

You don't believe an alcoholic is going to abandon his bottle or that a cripple will get his missing limb back. How can I keep waiting for him to love me, and above all for him to be able to say it—in his incapacity to love?

An implacable uncertainty makes me forge on with life whichever way I can. I putter about: I stagnate. I am a stagnant mass. That's all there is to it. He'll never love me. At least, he doesn't love me yet. I'm persuaded that if he loved me he'd be plunged into a madness much like mine…

He'd always be hanging on me, stalking me, suspecting me of things, tearing me on the edges of his powerful jealousy, his unhealthy, immeasurable jealousy.

All in all, this is how I know he doesn't love me. If he were in love he would act like a crazy person—and, up till now, and for ages, he hasn't shown any bizarre reactions. Hardly even violent.

If I let him, he'd massacre me. And then ask for forgiveness. In his murderous violence he'd like to disfigure me, mutilate me, make me gag—and while attacking, bearing down on my mouth while I struggle to clench my teeth, he'd shove his finger in. While he's yanking my hair, his thrashing blinds me, his words are like fireworks.

And then he washes my body, even between my legs, checking the temperature of the water, without wetting my face—so that my eyes keep their beauty, adorned in their tints, making sure he finds an immaculate towel, and it has to be a white one.

He would have preferred a virgin. I know. I sincerely regret not being a virgin when he took me for the first time, whatever pleasures I've had along the way—either before him or with him.

He finds me beautiful; my chest really is, and no one's skin is as soft as mine. My instincts are fantastic—so, in sum, he asks, why am I ready to die for him? But my transfiguration came only with my love for him, the moment that his instinct for beauty recognized my beauty, and recognized it in its unevenness—able to go from repulsive plainness to the most captivating loveliness. My breasts have become beautiful under his gaze, also because I no longer fold my arms over them, in shame and embarrassment, thinking they're too far apart. He has reassured me in my femininity and confirmed me in the blazing of my perceptions. This is probably because he's so attentive to what I tell him.
"Look at me, I am nothing,
Look closely at me..."
he says, summing himself up. I'm wounded, and I hurt for him if he really thinks that. He is handsome and above all he moves me. The sadness in his eyes speaks to me of the finiteness of all the universes. How could this still water, so alive, so radiant, one day liquefy in putrefaction in a shriveled and rigid corpse?
The trouble in his eyes means there's nothing to believe in, nothing to hope for, that even the sun, one day, will burn through an eternal night. The night that your gaze holds, along with your glory and the light you have been for me...

In those moments when I'm slapping him like a sadistic animal, I catch his gaze and we seem to be saying to each other that, by killing each other, we might resolve everything—us, our children, our contradictions along with the fact that we are mortal and thus our affair has made elite beings of us, demi-gods, geniuses...

We are not really what's extraordinary, it's the extraordinary nature of the bonds we have that transcends us, making a poem out of these bonds, a murder, a cosmic relativity, a tragedy and a rainbow above a steeped earth giving off steam.

"But if you don't love me,
Why do you keep after me...?"
"It's your pussy I want,
What I want is to fuck you."

He is terribly soft, and insidiously dangerous.

Chapter V

What opens before us is still the choice of life or death. We could have a child which I would name one of those names that are deep with memory for him—memory of his soft, acute and strange language. That language of unknown origin and lost writing. When women sing in that language the songs are surely the most beautiful in the world. Their raucous voices explode from their chests, an emptying, a narrative of the difficulty of being.

I have not had my share of maternity, and he has not been anointed the perfect dad, serene, calm, and serious. It's not from two lacks that we would have created a child—but from two talents that were never really tried. Intact and complementary.

You can't be a mother all by yourself, or a father either; it's unfair. That was our trial. A child to be shared with one or the other parent, but not both, even when they're together in their parallel and singularly different worlds.

We were those children—and we had those children. We could never perfect ourselves alone, and within each other, without that grand crusade of having a child with the loved one. More than that, it would be the Assumption of two beings, their coronation of each other. I have this feeling—it's so full and heavy—when our eyes meet and when we kiss each other's hands: that's what it is to create a child.

When you're both far from and very close to no longer being able to do anything—that is to learn, seduce, give birth—you regret so much not having that vast energy to grab everything you can from the void and bend it toward the flow of life. But our weakness resides in the bare fact of already being my age, in being his age. When what we would need is the power of a colossus and the charging of a wild beast.

Perhaps the all-consuming desire to have a child with this man is nothing but my immense interior void revealed in a whirlwind. If I weren't so empty, would I love such a cold man?

For him, I'm that leaning toward an exasperated quivering that he has felt so strongly—and that he has never, in his whole life, stopped silencing and blocking, never having found the chance to let it all come alive.

We humans suffer so much from poor communication that I could erect myriad systems and hypothetical explanations about him and I'd still only be groping my way and getting things wrong.

To tell the truth, I don't even understand my overboard feelings for him and all this unhealthy attachment.

Three months ago I'd gone several weeks without seeing him. I'd become strung out, haggard, yellow in complexion, emaciated. I sweated despair from every pore and was headed downhill in every sense. He finally agreed to see me. I trembled before him, half-collapsed in a soft chair. I was so weak that I sank to the floor, feeling that I'd have less to bear that way.

He saw I wasn't alright. Anyone could tell.

He made love to me. At those times, our coming together is always the same—a playing over again, whole and identical. That's what many people wouldn't get. Before our affair, I didn't know much either, about love.

After my special union with him, a fusion that surrounded everything else with its incandescence, he had become essential to me, and, despite everything he might say, I'm a kind of flower as yet unopened for him, because he senses that this is the first time I'm caught up in this region of fire and passion.

At the instant of our fusion we both know how strong it is, and that it's destined to last forever, even if nothing outside of it can reach this level.

The braziers in which our bodies writhe are the very source of whatever will save us...

He took note—silently—of my somber clothes, my face scarred by suffering. He stated that he was leaving, for one of our rendezvous spots, in fact. And it felt as though a weight were pressing down on my shoulders. I wasn't ready to go on such a long trip, all in the same day... He wanted to leave me, and I was absolutely unable to bear it. I started crying. Then, thinking I was about to blubber, I fled to another room, out of his sight. And there I heaved great sobs, no longer caring what he might think or feel about it. I wept like a woman lost forever. He tried to console me, awkwardly. I felt as though my heart had been hacked apart. On the doorsill I told him I didn't want to see him anymore, that it was over, that one of us should just go to Hell.

And that same evening, perked up again, happily back in harness, wrapped in the old spirit of luxury—which doesn't wash away the sadness but only makes it worse—I took the same plane as he, and spent one of the most beautiful days and nights of my life in his company.

He was patient, available, smiling, funny even. There he was again—a good dinner companion, an exquisite friend for walks, feasts. I was getting visibly thinner, right in front of him. I hardly touched my food. I didn't sleep at night even though he was by my side. I was—how do you put this—strung so tight I was ready to snap, like a cord that can't vibrate any tighter. Like glass that a very high note will shatter.

I rose from our bed around three or four o'clock in the morning, still sleepless. We had made love with our unique conviction, our way of giving and expecting nothing in return. The other person is all-important. I'm only the servant who rushes to give him a little, or a little more, or all the happiness a human could ever accept without going crazy or dying from it.

The next day I went out to get tranquilizers around noon. He didn't understand, and yet it was so simple—I felt so good it was unbearable. I was likely to burst something inside.

We made love again. And then some more. After too much of this I was spread out at his feet, in red and black, dressed up again to take off, because this intense happiness was beginning to scare me. I don't know why he came at me all over again, at the end of this low bed; all he had to do was slightly lift a flap of black cloth.

He could see my stomach and this made him crazy—he entered me, trembling:

"You're going to kill me…"

It was two people dying together in a slowly depleted love, hearts beating with exhaustion, temples pounding. Has anyone ever had such a chance, at closeness, at flight?

He must live with me, he must—so that I don't die from losing him. Him—who says our story might end in death. I will give up ever seeing this child we bear in us, who will exist or not, depending—from one minute to the next—on my wish. All I need is this man's presence every day, his gaze, his silence, and us, till the end. That is, a beautiful death, the death of two old people.

His indiscreet look that understands all, about people and things, the knots on his fragile hands, the slenderness of his body, that innate distinction of his, an air of weariness so hard for him to mask—and him, like my mirror, me like his reflection.

We are each other's myths, Gemini of our shadows and silences. We want to survive in each other.

Beyond time, our affair has not been spoiled in the wear and tear of time, of couples, of too much sex or too many kisses given and enjoyed.

His shy resistance to everyday things took its toll on our affair; instead of pulling away from the mistress he'd beheld too much, he began to draw near and to be her double, her twin, her prey and torturer. The roles became fluid and changing, because gentleness, complicity, and an exaggerated tenderness—refused but indwelling—bade them kiss each other's hands in a sign of allegiance, affability, and courtesy.

Their affair is so particular to them that it's only possible when they're together as two; when I'm not with him I become single again in every way, and I speak of these two as if the I that exists *with him* is an I that becomes part of a whole—and finally has meaning. Away from him, I become, once again, attempts. Attached to him, I'm like the full moon, the floodtide and the female drawing near to her male.

If only life is merciful to us and allows a union beyond our affair and this fusing together, and against the separation that can no longer be—but which of us will accept the companion's dying first, and being there to see it... my Eyes?

~~*Summer, 1985*

Epilogue

Tywalyne's husband very soon became old—an attack felled him like a many-rooted oak ripped out of the ground by a hurricane. The eagle was now nothing but a bird in the hands of sadistic children who lose interest only when their object is half-dead.

This is how Tywalyne came to love him no longer...

Acknowledgments

Rita El Khayat's conversations were as indulgent as they were illuminating. The translator is more grateful than ever for the patient and expert work of editor Anna Bliss.

Dernières parutions

LES BLESSURES DE L'ABSENCE
Oran, 5 juillet 1962 - Roman
Claude Diaz
Ce roman est un hymne au courage de quatre femmes, de générations différentes, confrontées aux turpitudes de l'absence. Les parcours divergents de leur époux révèlent la complexité des engagements dans la guerre d'Algérie qui les broie. À travers le destin de Norbert, le roman rend hommage aux disparus du conflit algérien.
(Coll. Rue des écoles, 23 euros, 262 p., octobre 2017)
EAN : 9782343122823 EAN PDF : 9782140048395

LES CAROUBES DE MOSTAGANEM
Roman
Gabriel Sebban
À l'aube des «Événements», l'Algérie dévoile son désir d'indépendance. Les Malset, des Pieds-noirs bien établis, lèguent à leur fille la ferme florale des Caroubes. La guerre qui s'installe dans la période 1955-59 transforme les relations, interroge les attachements et les valeurs. Les conflits intra et intercommunautaires s'accentuent et entrechoquent les générations. Ce milieu du XXe siècle confronte les personnes à des choix cornéliens où le devoir, la transmission des aînés et le respect de l'humain peinent à s'harmoniser.
(Coll. Ethnographiques, 19,5 euros, 204 p., octobre 2017)
EAN : 9782343128634 EAN PDF : 9782140046599

LE SERMENT DU FIGUIER
Roman
Hamid Boukrif
La quête d'une identité pour une communauté nationale est un parcours historique difficile, le renforcement du système de valeurs qui sous-tend cette ambition collective est primordiale. L'héritage est intergénérationnel et l'engagement de chacun des membres conforte la légitimité d'une existence faite de solidarité et de tolérance. C'est le message que veut faire passer l'auteur à travers l'histoire singulière d'un patriarche centenaire, guide éclairé de sa communauté, soucieux de sa cohésion et des liens du sang de ses membres.
(Coll. Lettres du monde arabe, 21,5 euros, 242 p., octobre 2017)
EAN : 9782343110073 EAN PDF : 9782140048586

YOUMMA
Roman
Ahmed Saïfi Benziane
Au retour d'une soirée au clair de lune, Aïssa traverse un ancien cimetière pour rejoindre son domicile. Il y croise une image du destin qui va bouleverser sa vie et remettre en cause toutes les certitudes de la vie. Il découvre alors des valeurs insoupçonnées chez les êtres les plus proches, mais aussi chez des personnes qu'il est forcé de rencontrer dans sa quête de vérité.
(Harmattan Algérie, 19 euros, 190 p., octobre 2017)
EAN : 9782343131221 EAN PDF : 9782140048340

UN RÊVE ENDEUILLÉ
Fatima El Bouanani
Horria est une jeune femme de 29 ans, épouse d'une personnalité militaire pesante et mère de deux filles. En dépit d'une vie luxueuse, elle mène une existence pitoyable, maltraitée par un mari qui l'enferme et l'aliène. Devenant étrangère à elle-même, à ses filles et à la vie, elle réussit à développer une indifférence envers les êtres et les choses. Sur Facebook, elle fait la connaissance d'Amine, un universitaire. L'amour naissant entre eux va profondément modifier la froideur de cette existence, lui ouvrant grandes les portes du rêve, de la liberté et de l'espoir.
(Coll. Lettres du monde arabe, 17,5 euros, 160 p., septembre 2017)
EAN : 9782343110431 EAN PDF : 9782140044526

L'AFFAIRE MEURSAULT
Roman
Michel Thouillot
Et si Meursault avait obtenu du jury les circonstances atténuantes pour le meurtre d'un « Arabe » dans une Algérie dominée ? S'il avait échappé à la peine capitale pour plonger dans l'enfer carcéral ? Derrière les barreaux, le héros de Camus serait en butte à la justice rendue par les détenus indigènes et assisterait à la montée du nationalisme algérien. Il serait alors amené à des révisions déchirantes, mais tardives... L'auteur réinvente ici librement *L'Étranger* pour éclairer l'envers du décor d'une colonie engagée sur la voie de l'implosion.
(17 euros, 162 p., juillet 2017)
EAN : 9782343121864 EAN PDF : 9782140041372

LE GÉNÉRAL K
Roman
Mustapha Yalaoui
Le Général K est dérangé dans sa retraite forcée par le lieutenant Damraoui, venu lui annoncer la désertion de Mourad Mellali, ancien du bureau des investigations. Trahison ? Duplicité ? Opération scabreuse ? Dans une Algérie meurtrie par la guerre civile, par des vagues d'attentats endeuillant le pays, par un État au bord de l'effondrement, le Général K va parvenir, entre Alger et Constantine, à rassembler les indices édifiants de la machination fomentée dans l'esprit aliéné d'une petite poignée d'hommes assoiffés de pouvoir et de sang.
(Coll. Lettres du monde arabe, 26,5 euros, 312 p., juillet 2017)
EAN : 9782343122755 EAN PDF : 9782140041693

BAS-FONDS DE LA HAINE
Brahim Korib
Quelque peu colorée, la vie amère de l'enfance de l'auteur demeure authentique et aussi idyllique qu'une perle perdue dans les décombres de l'enfer. L'histoire d'amour relatée dans ce roman n'est que le fantasme d'un cœur meurtri violemment par les atrocités de la guerre. Elle demeure purement fictive, même si elle est inspirée de certains faits réels.
(Coll. Lettres du monde arabe, 21,5 euros, 254 p., juin 2017)
EAN : 9782343123387 EAN PDF : 9782140039577

LE FAUX BARRAGE
Hamid Benchaar
De retour dans son pays d'origine après une longue absence, le narrateur de ce roman retrouve un pays encore traumatisé par le conflit armé qu'il vient de vivre. Ayant échappé à la mort lors d'un faux barrage, Omar est amené à s'interroger sur les raisons qui ont poussé les terroristes à l'épargner. Des questions, puis des doutes, le conduisent à se pencher sur le passé de son père, héros national, et des événements qui ont secoué la région des Aurès pendant la lutte pour l'indépendance. Ce texte est un voyage dans les méandres et les contradictions de la nouvelle société algérienne, en quête de son identité, mais victime d'une amnésie organisée.
(Coll. Lettres du monde arabe, 15 euros, 144 p., juin 2017)
EAN : 9782343119137 EAN PDF : 9782140038808

LE COUPABLE
Hassan Banhakeia
Fuyant les misères africaines, le jeune Sembratiri émigre clandestinement à Paris. Il y rencontre Jeanne, plus âgée que lui. Ils mènent une vie de couple difficile, lui qui aime tant jouer à la machine à sous... Accusé injustement du meurtre de la Française, il s'enfuit et arrive par miracle à s'échapper vers l'Afrique. Sur les pas du coupable se lance l'inspecteur Saintmuté qui veut à tout prix lui faire payer des crimes qu'il n'a jamais commis. En collusion avec les autorités indigènes, l'inspecteur français cerne Sembratiri qui se voit perdu...
(Coll. Écritures, 22 euros, 264 p., juin 2017)
EAN : 9782343120782 EAN PDF : 9782140039881

LES ÉPINES DES ROSES
Khalil Mgharfaoui
Idir découvre dans l'ordinateur de son père, Meddur, tombé dans le coma, des textes où celui-ci parle de sa vie, de sa maladie et de son amour pour Tayri. En lisant ces textes, Idir découvre peu à peu un père qu'il ne connaissait pas : ses doutes, ses peurs, sa fragilité et son grand amour de jeunesse. Ému par ces découvertes, il décide de partir à la recherche de la seule personne que son père n'ait jamais aimée.
Coll. Lettres du monde arabe, avril 2017, 272 pages, 23.50 euros
ISBN : 978-2-343-11722-5 / EAN PDF : 9782140034824

LIGNE DE FUITE
Djamal Satour
«La ville découvrait une géographie secrète et des courants inconnus. Elle se montrait porteuse d'une évocation invitant à changer de regard. Une autre réalité

était en train de filtrer. Alors, comme en réaction et pour brouiller la vision, l'atmosphère se tendait et la situation s'agitait. Des vagues de violence se mettaient ensuite à déferler. Les choses devenaient incompréhensibles. Rien ne semblait plus relever du hasard...». Ce roman évoque l'atmosphère à Alger au début des années 1990, alors que la ville est en proie à la violence terroriste.
(Coll. Lettres du monde arabe, 17,5 euros, 146 p., janvier 2017)
EAN : 9782343106250 EAN PDF : 9782140026027

L'APATRIDE
Nasser Chali
Le récit retrace le retour d'un immigré chez lui après une très longue absence. Il constate à son arrivée que tout a changé et qu'il n'arrive plus à retrouver ses repères. Il deviendra donc un orphelin de pays, un apatride, coupé de ses racines, qui cherche malgré tout à retrouver sa place. «Notre foule frustrée était à la merci de n'importe quel charlatan pourvu qu'il parle bien et effleure la vérité. Les gens étaient alors prêts à le suivre quel qu'en soit le prix. Quel gâchis dans un si beau pays. Mais cela va de soi. Quand un pays est orphelin de son Histoire, il se fabrique des héros, fussent-ils de pacotille.»
(Coll. Lettres du monde arabe, 19,5 euros, 202 p., janvier 2017)
EAN : 9782343101811 EAN PDF : 9782140026669

BLESSURES DES MOTS
Journal de Tunisie
Wounding Words. A Woman's Journal in Tunisia
Édition bilingue
Evelyne Accad
Traduit en anglais par Cynthia T. Hahn
Voici «un livre pionnier qui a bien su montrer toutes les facettes du mouvement des femmes tunisiennes et par là même des femmes arabes dans ce qu'il a de plus révolutionnaire pour la société, un rôle qui est apparu de manière encore plus évidente lors de la révolution tunisienne de 2011» (Georges Corm). L'auteure nous dévoile la vie intérieure déchirante d'une jeune femme libanaise au cours d'une année passée en Tunisie. Aux heures tragiques d'aujourd'hui, ce récit nous apprend que, du côté des femmes arabes, une révolution en sommeil attend toujours et encore son heure. (Édition française, Indigo-Côté femmes, 2014).
(Coll. Créations au féminin, 25 euros, 290 p., janvier 2017)
EAN : 9782343108094 EAN PDF : 9782140025624

LA ROUTE DE TAMANRASSET
Denis Fontaine
Largement inspiré de son propre voyage, l'auteur nous conte l'histoire d'un jeune homme qui s'embarque pour Alger au milieu des années 1980, muni d'un vélo et d'une tente, afin de rallier Tamanrasset. Le récit de sa randonnée d'oasis en oasis, à hauteur d'homme, fait revivre au présent cette Algérie saharienne, grandiose, belle et fraternelle. Au bout du voyage, le narrateur met ses pas dans ceux de Charles de Foucauld, jusqu'au plateau de l'Assekrem. Il rend ainsi hommage à cet ermite du Hoggar, fondateur involontaire de Tamanrasset, où il mourut le 1er décembre 1916.
(21 euros, 234 p., décembre 2016)
EAN : 9782343104379 EAN PDF : 9782140023866